SHAKY TOWN

A NOVEL

story—sometimes brutal, often unrequited, but never dishonest."

> —J. Ryan Stradal, author of *The Lager Queen of Minnesota* and *Kitchens of the Great Midwest*

"For years now, Lou Mathews has written with a luscious urgency, as though he's telling secrets he promised not to. *Shaky Town* is a particular triumph of storytelling, crackling with its own distinct energy and intelligence. The characters are jumpy at the margins—volatile, mournful, funny as hell—with the little-known warrens and alleyways of Los Angeles teeming all around them. Mathews is a master, and perhaps contemporary fiction's best-kept secret."

> —Claire Vaye Watkins, author of *Battleborn* and *Gold Fame Citrus*

"With *Shaky Town,* Lou Mathews brings a fascinating and unforgettable corner of the real Los Angeles to vivid life, creating an authentic portrait of a time, a place, and a people. This community is no stranger to tragedy and loss, but there is much beauty, hope, and even humor in Mathews's stories as well. His characters know what it means to endure, to survive. They have their triumphs and their struggles—yet so often in these pages, if we pay close enough attention, they are also showing us how to live."

> —Skip Horack, author of *The Other Joseph* and *The Eden Hunter*

A NOVEL

Lou Mathews

TIGER VAN BOOKS

Published by Tiger Van Books,
an imprint of Prospect Park Books/Turner Publishing
www.turnerpublishing.com

Hardcover: 9781735303802

Paperback: 9781684428083

Ebook: 9781684428236

Library of Congress Control Number: 2021939569

Some of these chapters were published as stories in the following magazines and anthologies: *Black Clock, Crazyhorse, Failbetter, Los Angeles Reader, Short Story, The Rattling Wall, UCLA Quarterly, Witness, ZYZZYVA, The Best of Failbetter, The Black Clock Mix Tape, Fiction Gallery, L.A. Shorts, Portales, The Pushcart Prize,* and *Love Stories for the Rest of Us: The Best of the Pushcart Prize.* The novella *Shaky Town,* which won *Failbetter*'s tenth anniversary novella contest, was originally published in *Failbetter* under the title *The Irish Sextet.*

All graffiti in *Con Safos Rifa* was inked by the author.

The writer would like to acknowledge and thank the National Endowment for the Arts and the California Arts Commission for their encouragement and support.

Cover design by Stephen ESPO Powers
Book layout and design by Amy Inouye, Future Studio

Printed in the United States of America

For my Aunt Dorothy and Uncle Jesús Renteria

Thank you for your stories.
Forgive me for not telling them as well as you did.

CONTENTS

EMILIANO PART I: THE MAYOR PROCLAIMS

I WAS TALKING to one of my constituents this morning, but he didn't know it. George was his name, I didn't learn that until later. He didn't know he was a constituent, he didn't know I was the Mayor, he didn't know he was sitting in my office.

He thought it was a bus bench, there at the corner of Fletcher Avenue and San Fernando Road. He didn't even know he was a citizen of Shaky Town. He thought he lived in some city called Los Angeles. That's where you reside, I told him. ¡You live in Shaky Town! Shaky Town is what goes on around you. It's your neighborhood, your barrio, and that's much more important than any imaginary city. He didn't know what a barrio was.

I looked at him, this well-dressed double-breasted man, classic in a charcoal stripe with a tie the color of the bleeding sacred candy apple heart, and I smiled. Buenos días, I told him, Cómo está? He said he didn't speak Spanish.

I told him what I said was Good morning and How

are you? and I introduced myself, Emiliano Gomez, a sus ordenes—at your service—and you are? That was when I learned his name was George, George Thibodeaux, and his family was from New Orleans and he didn't speak Spanish and he said he didn't need to speak Spanish because he was a Black man. I said, Well, you're a little darker than me, but not much, and you could be from Mexico. It was your mustache that fooled me, they grow them that way in Zacatecas. That exact style with the razor edge. And I told him, But you do speak Spanish. He said, No, I don't. I said, But you do. That made him straighten his tie.

You know burrito. You know taco. Enchilada. Maybe even chile relleno. Or carnitas. He started to laugh. He said, That doesn't count.

I said, Don't laugh. That's part of the language. If you want to eat well, you learn the language. Why do you think the Spanish were conquered by the Mexicans? He picked up his briefcase then and looked at me like I was crazy. He said, What? That's crazy. I said, But they were. You have to look at the final outcome. Not just one battle. I know. I'm a student of history.

Look at Napoleon, I told him. Napoleon used to say, An army travels on its stomach. He said that while his troops were eating their horses. But who could blame them? The Russians had no chiles.

And how much better are the Russians today for winning? There's a better way to win. An army can be conquered by its stomach. It's true. Look at Mexico and here.

In the United States, the native peoples, the ones we call Indians, were wiped out. Their lands were taken from them. They disappeared. How many Indians, among 250 million people, are left? One percent? Maybe.

In Mexico, ninety-five percent of the population is still Indio or mixed blood. The Spanish got absorbed. The difference is the food. What did Estados Unidos Indians have to offer their conquerors? Fried bread and dried meat. Jerky. That was the peak of their cuisine. Good for rednecks maybe. Nobody else wanted to eat it. Also, because they had no chiles, they were susceptible to European diseases.

In Mexico it was different. Those conquistadors, raised on bread and cheese and meat, saw for the first time mangoes, papaya, guavas, potatoes, tomatoes, avocados, bananas, pineapples, fruits that had no name, and thirty kinds of chiles. Monkeys threw mangoes at their helmets. There was corn, which no one could explain. They saw corn tortillas, enchiladas. ¡Tamales!

No one who has ever eaten a truly good tamale can be a conqueror. Those conquistadors were helpless. They had to marry those cooks instead of killing them. There was too much to lose. Even what they brought was improved. They brought wheat and beer. We made flour tortillas and better beer than anyone ever drank in Spain. You ever been there? The beer there is terrible. To this day. That's why you can speak Spanish. So you can order a good Mexican beer, a Bohemia or a Carta Blanca. That's Bowe-aye-mee-haa. Or Dos Equis, although with that one you can just hold up two Xs and they know. Stay away from Tecate.

George held his hand up. He said, Are you a teacher? I said, No, I'm the Mayor, but I can tell when someone needs education. That made him straighten his tie again.

So the food is a start, I told him.

Where do you live? I asked. What is your street?

Ahh, Salsipuedes Street. You prove my point.

Half the streets in L.A. are Spanish. Salsipuedes is actually three words. Sal Si Puedes. It means Get out if you can! I don't know why they called your street that. In Mexico, they put that sign on the worst places.

You're right. It is interesting. Only seven o'clock in the morning and already you've learned something. You could take the day off, que no?

That means, Why not? It's the second-most Mexican expression.

The first? Quién sabe? Quién sabe? That means Who knows? You have to say it with a shrug. You say it like a question, but it's not really a question. Everybody knows that nobody knows. It's telling God how small you are. The world laughs at you, you can't laugh back—that might offend the world—but you can shrug your shoulders, maybe smile a little, and say, Quién sabe?

George looked at me. He said, Like in *The Lone Ranger*?

No. No. That's different. Tonto said, Kemo Sabe. I never thought about that before. Maybe that is the Indian version. He's telling the Lone Ranger, Who knows? That would make sense.

I knew him. Jay Silverheels. Tonto. Jay Silverheels was his real name. He was a fine man. He always talked to me on the set. I worked in the movie business for twelve years. First Warner's, then MGM. I was a carpenter. Breakaways were my specialty. Whenever you see John Wayne break a chair over someone's head? I built that chair. Balsa wood, stained dark, all hand carved. You couldn't put balsa in a lathe. When someone got thrown out of a window? I built that window. Balsa frames, sugar-glass panes. You're right. It was a strange job. I was an artisan, I did beautiful work, so someone could break it. Twenty chairs, all exactly alike, because they might need twenty takes to get it right. You never knew. If Juan Grande Pendejo was hungover that day, or he didn't like the other actor, he might break all twenty. The director would let him. Better to have Frankie Avalon crying than John Grande mad at you. How many Westerns was Frankie Avalon going to make? So another twenty chairs. That job did a funny thing to me. I never made any real furniture. Not for myself or for any of my family.

Then I lost these three fingers. Yeah, I saw you looking. All but the little one. I can still make the horns. No, it's okay. You can ask. I cut them off. Two inches of white pine slat and three fingers of bone. I measured wrong. It was supposed to be three inches of pine and no fingers. The table saw didn't care.

I was drunk. It couldn't be helped. My oldest had died.

Carlos. Mi Carlitos. Ten years old, the polio. I stayed up all night drinking with the priest, Father McNulty. He didn't have any answers. So I went to work. What else was there to do? Quién sabe, no? Pride can be a bad thing. It cost me that job, these fingers.

That's not true. It's true about the fingers, but Garcia cost me that job. The studio would have found something else for me. But Garcia, that Garcia, he had a boy he wanted to get into the union. That's the one trouble with the movies. Everybody wants to get their kids in. So he told them I was drunk. They asked me, I couldn't lie. Bang, out the door.

The insurance company, when they heard, they wouldn't pay me. They sued me for the doctor and the hospital, too. Companies could do that stuff then.

So I was out the door. I had the disability, but it wasn't good for me. It gave me too much time and money to drink. I got bitter. You do that when you have the time. It's like actors. I was around them a lot. Actors are the best people in the world. As long as they're working. When they aren't working, they have time to think about the injustice of the world. Particularly where it concerns them. They go crazy.

They should say, Quién sabe? But they don't. I was like that. I turned my back on God. I thought, He's turning his back to me, why shouldn't I turn my back to him? We had a fine priest then, that one I mentioned, Father McNulty. He liked his whiskey, which is a good thing in a priest. But even Father McNulty couldn't tell me why God would let Carlitos die.

My friend Esteban was wiser than God or Father McNulty then. At least, he knew what I needed. He got me on where he worked. The City of Beverly Hills, trash collecting. Twenty-eight years I worked there. I retired three years ago, and last year I decided to become Mayor. No, I know you didn't vote. It was by acclamation. Everybody is allowed to vote in Shaky Town, even ghosts and the animals, too. All the animals voted for me, they still do, the roosters every morning, the birds all day, and the dogs and coyotes at night. Put your head outside sometime. You can hear them vote.

I'm talking too much. I'm sorry. You get caught up in your life, you think it should mean something to somebody else.

You would rather know when your bus gets here, am I right?

You want downtown? You just missed the local. The express will be here in tres minutos. So you're better off, you'll beat the local by twenty minutes. The only disadvantage is me. And I can shut up. Thank you. You're polite. You're right, you have some time, I'll tell you about it.

Twenty-eight years. It doesn't seem so long to me. It was a good place to work, Beverly Hills. I showed up the first day wearing rubber gloves. Esteban was worried about my hand. So I wore rubber gloves, and I stuffed clay in the empty fingers. Nobody figured it out. For the first couple of years nobody knew they were missing.

One day on the route, I cut the glove on some sheet metal. They were doing some new air-conditioning on a house. I picked up the old ducts that they'd cut out, the edges were like razors. I couldn't feel it when those fake fingers got snagged. One, two of them dropped off onto the sidewalk. I'll never forget my partner. Ivory Eakins was his name. As nice a man as ever lived. He died eight years ago. Ivory dropped his can, looking at me, and let it roll into the street. His face turned gray and he said, Emiliano? Your hand! I looked down and I saw what he saw. Fingers rolling down the street. I shrugged. I said, We Mexicans are tough. Especially from Zacatecas. Then I sliced off the last fake finger on the metal, tossed it in the trash can, and Ivory fainted.

He didn't forgive me for a long time, but it was still worth it. The word got around to the boss, but by then I'd proved I could do the job. Twenty-eight years. Goes by like your bus. You get on, you get off.

When I retired, I decided I should be the Mayor here

because I have seniority. I moved here in 1922. I was five years old. Nobody else has lived here longer. Mrs. Espinosa will argue with you, but I can remember when she moved here. It was 1928. Before that she lived in Frogtown. She counts that, but Frogtown is across the tracks.

That doesn't count. This is Shaky Town.

I'll tell you how long I've been here. After the earthquake in 1923, when the dam broke, this street was flooded to the tops of the trees. Right where we're sitting, I floated over it on a raft, in 1923. I tied that raft to an orange tree, right across the street. There was a whole grove then, where the pallet factory is now.

So you're learning what a wonderful barrio you live in. Historical. That bakery was built in 1930, and Shaky Town has smelled good ever since. That drive-in opened in 1945. It's the best example of Streamline Moderne architecture in California.

I come down at night sometimes just to look at it. It's beautiful, all lit up, the carhops on roller skates, and the windmill blades turning.

I bring a copita of brandy and sit here across the street and sip, and I think, Emiliano, you're just like the Quixote. He had his windmills and you have yours. Only yours have neon lights!

That's enough history for one day. You should know about where you live. Now you get to go to work and you've learned something. Don't laugh. You should learn something new every day. It's like the bankers say, Pay yourself first. Put something into savings before you pay your bills. Here comes your bus.

CRAZY LIFE

CHUEY CALLED ME from the jail. He said it was all a big mistake. I said, Sure, Chuey, like always, que no? What is it this time, weed or wine? He said it was something different this time. I said, You mean like reds, angel dust, what? Chuey said, No Dulcie, something worse.

I said, So? Why call me? Why don't you call that Brenda who was so nice to you at the party? He said, Dulcie. Listen. It's a lot worse. I got to get a lawyer. Then he like started to cry or something. Not crying, Chuey wouldn't cry, but it was like he had a hard time breathing. I couldn't believe it. I didn't do it, Dulcie, he told me. I didn't do nothing. I was just in the car.

I got scared then. Chuey, I said, can anybody hear you? He said there was a chota around and some dude from the DA's office, but not close. I told him, Shut up, Chuey. Just shut up. Don't say nothing to nobody. I'll come down. Chuey said, I don't know if they'll let you see me.

They'll let me, I said. Hang on.

I skipped school, fifth and sixth periods, just gym and home wreck, and hitchhiked up to Highland Park. I been there before, the Highland Park cop shop. Chuey has been busted there three or four times. Nothing bad, just drunk and one time a joint in the car.

This time it looked bad. They had a bunch of reporters there. This TV chick was on the steps when I come up, standing in front of the bright lights saying about the police capturing these guys. She kept saying the same words, Drive-by murders. Drive-by murders. There was these two kids, brothers, and one was dead and the other was critical.

I walked up the steps, and all these people started yelling. This one guy tells me, You can't come up here while we're shooting. I told him, You don't own the steps. The TV lights go out and the chick with the microphone says, Fuck. Then she turns around to me, real sarcastic and says, Thanks a lot, honey. I told her, Chinga tu madre, bitch, I got rights, too. My boyfriend's in there. I got more business here than you. She gave me the big eyes and went to complain to her boss.

I went on inside, up to the desk, and said, I'm here to see Chuey Medina. Who? he says, and he looks at the list. We got a Jesús Medina. That's Chuey, I tell him.

He looks at me, up and down, this fat Paddy with the typical little cop mustache. What's your name, he says. Dulcie Medina, I tell him. It's not, but if they don't think we're related they won't let me see Chuey. Dulcie? he says, Does that mean sugar? Sweet, I tell him, it means sweet.

You related? he says. What the hell, I'm thinking, God can't get me till I get outside. I tell him, I'm his wife.

Well, sweetheart, he says, nobody gets to see Jesús Medina until he's been booked. He says it Jeezus, not Hayzhoos, like he's making a big point.

He's *been* booked, I say. He called me. They wouldn't have let him call me if he hadn't been booked already. The cop looks real snotty at me, but he knows I'm right. Just a minute, he says. He gets on the phone. When he gets off, he says, You'll have to wait. You can wait over there.

How long? I say. He gets snotty again. I don't know, sweetheart, he says. They'll call me.

Cops when they don't know what to do, they know to make you wait. I hung out, smoking, for a while. Outside on the steps, the lights are on and that same blond TV bitch is holding a microphone up to a guy in a suit. He's banging his briefcase against his knee while he talks. I come out the door as the guy is saying, We have to send a message to gang members that we will no longer tolerate—blah, blah, blah, like that—and then all this stuff about the community.

Hey, I tell him, are you the DA? They won't let me see my husband, Chuey Medina. He turns around. The blondie is mouthing at me GO AWAY. I tell the DA guy, They won't let him talk to a lawyer. Isn't he entitled to legal representation? Those are magic words. He grabs me by the arm. Mrs. Medina, he says, let's talk inside. The blondie jerks a thumb across her throat and the lights go out. She looks at me and thinks of something. Keep rolling, she says, and the lights go on again. Mrs. Medina, she says, Mrs. Medina. Could we talk with you a moment? The DA still has hold of my arm, and he pulls me through the door. She gives him a nasty look and then turns around to the lights again. I can hear her as we're going through the door.

In a dramatic development, she says, here at the Highland Park Police Station, the wife of alleged drive-by murderer Jesús "Chuey" Medina has accused the district attorney's office…. The DA says, Goddamnit. I don't hear what she says after that, my legs get like water, and he has to help me over to the bench. Chuey didn't kill nobody, I tell him. He wouldn't. He looks at me funny, and I remember I'm supposed to already know everything. I straighten up and tell him, Chuey wants a lawyer.

That's simply not a problem, Mrs. Medina, he tells me. An attorney will be provided. I *know* Mr. Medina has been offered an attorney.

No, I say, he wanted a certain one. He told me on the phone, but your chingadera phone is such junk that I couldn't hear the name. I have to talk to him.

He gives me another funny look and goes over to the guy at the desk. Look, he tells the cop, I don't know what's going on here, but I don't want *any* procedural fuckups on this one.

The cop says, Big case, huh? and the DA tells him, This is the whole enchilada, Charlie. Where are you holding Medina?

Second-floor tank.

Okay, he says. We'll use the conference room there. Call ahead. The cop looks at me and tells the DA, We'll need a matron.

I know what that means. One time before, when I went to see my brother Carlos in jail, they gave me a strip search. It was some ugly shit. They put their fingers in everywhere, and I mean everywhere, and the lady who did it, she got off on it. You could tell. My ass was sore for a week. I swore to God I'd never let anybody do that to me again.

Bullshit, I yell. No strip search. The DA guy whirls around. The cop says, If it's a face-to-face meeting with a prisoner, the Captain says skin search. That's the way we play it.

The DA tells him, I'll take responsibility on this one. We'll do a pat search and I'll be with her every step after that. I'm going to walk this one through. He holds the cop on the arm. We got cameras out there, Charlie, he says.

The matron is waiting for me in this little room. Undo your blouse is the first thing she tells me. I already told them, I say, I ain't going to strip. Just the top two buttons, she says. Visual inspection, honey. I have to make sure your bra's not loaded.

I undo the buttons and hold the blouse open. Just some Kleenex, I tell her. She checks me out and then pats me down. Then she starts poking in my hair. They always do that. Some pachuca thirty years ago supposedly had a razor blade in her beehive and they're still excited about it. They never do it to any Anglo chicks.

The DA guy meets me outside, and we walk through the first-floor jail. It's like walking through the worst party you ever been to in your life. All these guys checking me out. Putting their hands through the bars and yelling. 'Ola, chica. Hey, chica, over here, they keep saying, and worse stuff. This one dude keeps making these really disgusting kissing noises. Guys can be weird. I give the dude the finger and make my walk all sexy on the way out, shaking my ass.

They all go wild. Serves them right.

Chuey is in this big cell, all by himself except for one other guy, and when I see who it is, I know why Chuey's in trouble. Sleepy Chavez is sitting next to him. I don't know why they call him Sleepy. He's wired most of the time. I think he might have been a red freak once. Sleepy is one vato loco, the craziest I know. Everything bad that happens on 42nd Avenue starts with Sleepy Chavez.

There's this guy that shines shoes outside Jesse's Barber Shop. I thought he was retarded, but it turns out he got in a fight with Sleepy in like sixth grade and Sleepy kicked him so hard in the huevos that the guy ain't been right since. And what's really sick is that Sleepy *loves* getting his shoes shined there.

Chuey doesn't look so good. He's got bruises on his cheeks, a cut on his forehead, and his hand's bandaged up. He looks like what the 42nd Flats, that's his gang, call resisting arrest. He looks sick, too, pale and his eyes are all red. Sleepy sees me first. He's chewing on his fingers, looks up, and spits out a fingernail. Sleepy can't leave his fingers alone. When he was little, his sister told me, his mom used to put chili juice on them. He's always poking them in his ears or picking his nose or something. You don't want to be alone with him.

Chuey stands up while the cop is unlocking the door. He just looks at me, and his eyes are so sad it makes me feel sick. He looks worse than when his father died or even when the guys from White Fence burned his car and laughed at him. Sleepy Chavez looks at me and chucks his head at Chuey. Watch your mouth, Medina, he says.

They take us into this big room. The cop stands by the door. The DA guy sits down at the end of this long table, and we go down to the other. Chuey reaches out and touches my face. Dulcie, he says. Mi novia. Chuey only calls me that when he's really drunk or sentimental. He never has asked me to marry him. No touching, the cop says, Keep your hands on the table. I figure Chuey needs cheering up, so I slip off my shoe and slide my foot up on the inside of his leg and rub him under the table.

Ay, Chuey, I tell him, all happy, Que problemas you have, Chuey. My toes are rubbing a certain place, but Chuey surprises me. He doesn't even push back.

Dulcie, he says, they think I was the shooter.

Keep your voice down, I say. What did you tell them? Exactamente.

We didn't say nothing. We got to stick together, like Sleepy says. They haven't got any witnesses.

Chuey, I say, one of those guys is still alive.

He sits up when I tell him that.

It doesn't matter, Chuey says. Neither of them saw us. All the cops got is Sleepy's car. They ain't got the gun. Sleepy threw it out when they were chasing us. Chuey, I said, were you driving? He just looks at me for a while and then he says, Yeah. I ask, How come you were driving?

He had the shotgun, Chuey said. I had to drive.

I can tell when Chuey's lying, which is most of the time. I think he was telling the truth. Chuey, I said, you're crazy. They'll put you both away. You don't owe Sleepy nothing.

Chuey looks mean at me, his eyes get all skinny. It was my fault we got caught, he says. We should have gotten away. I hit another car and wrecked Sleepy's Mustang. We tried to hide and the cops found us. I owe Sleepy, so just shut up, Dulcie.

It's hopeless to argue with Chuey when he gets like this. Muy macho. You can't talk to him about his friends, even the jerks. He won't believe me over them. Chuey says, I'm gonna need a good lawyer. Get me Nardoni.

Tony Nardoni is this big lawyer all the drug dealers in East LA use. Chuey, I say, I don't think Nardoni does this kind of stuff. I think he just does the drugs.

Yeah, he does, Chuey says. He's a lawyer, isn't he? Sometimes Chuey can be just as dumb as his friends. It's not even worth telling him. Now he's all puffed up. You call Nardoni, Chuey says, Tell him I'm a compañero of Flaco Valdez. Tell him we're like this—Chuey holds up two crossed fingers—tight. Flaco Valdez is like the heavy-duty drug dealer in Highland Park and Shaky Town. As usual, Chuey's bullshitting. Flaco never ran with the 42nd Flats and he deals mostly smack, so Chuey isn't even one of his customers. It's just that Flaco Valdez is the biggest name that Chuey can think of. Okay, I tell him, I'll call Nardoni. Now what about your mom?

Don't call her, Chuey says, all proud, I don't want her to know about this. Chuey, I say, Chuey you big estupido, she *is* going to hear about this. It's going to be in the papers and on TV.

Okay, Chuey says, like he's doing me this big favor, you can call her. Tell her they made a big mistake. Right, Chuey, I'm thinking. Smart, Chuey. Pretend it didn't happen, like always. That will be a fun phone call for me. His mom is going to go crazy.

I know better, but I have to ask. Chuey? I say. Why did you do such a stupid thing?

They was on our turf! Chuey says. They challenged us. Like we didn't have any huevos. We got huevos!

And whose smart idea was it to shoot those boys? As if I didn't know. Chuey just looks at me, he doesn't say nothing.

Chuey, I say, was you high? He looks down at the table. When he looks up again, I can't believe it, his eyes are wet. He sees me looking, so he closes them and just sits there with his eyes closed, pulling on his little chin beard. God, he's such a pretty dude. Ay, Dulcie, he says. His eyes open and he gives me that smile, the one I have to argue to get, the one I love him for. What can I say? Chuey tells me, La Vida Loca, no?

Right, Chuey, I think, La Vida Loca. The Crazy Life. It's the explanation for everything on 42nd Avenue.

The DA knocks on the table. Time, he says. I look right at him and I say, I got to talk to you. Chuey cuts his eyes at me, but I don't care. I never done anything like this, I never gone against him, but now I have to. Sleepy Chavez could give a shit if Chuey takes the fall. Chuey doesn't get it, he thinks he's tough. If he goes to a real jail, they'll bend him over. They'll fry those huevos of his that he's always talking about.

I walk over to the DA and sit down. I tell him, Sleepy Chavez was the shooter. Chuey was driving and he was stoned. If Chuey testifies, what will he get? That DA sees me for the first time. The numbers turn over in his eyes like a gas pump.

Mrs. Medina, he says, you are not a lawyer, I cannot

plea bargain with you. If you were a lawyer, I would probably tell you that your client is guilty and we can prove it.

You got some witnesses? I ask him. He doesn't say nothing, but the numbers start rolling again.

Chuey stands up and yells at me, Dulcie, you stupid bitch, just shut up. He's all pale and scared. The cop walks over and sits him down.

I'm going to get him a lawyer, I say. The DA tells me, If you get a lawyer, we will talk. I would say better sooner than later—he has this little smile—before a witness shows up.

One other thing, I tell him, If I was you, I'd put Chuey in a different cell from Sleepy Chavez.

Chuey won't kiss me goodbye. He pushes me away, all cold. He won't even look at me. Out in the hall, he won't look at Sleepy Chavez, either. Sleepy checks that out good, and then when he sees that the cop is taking Chuey someplace else, he starts banging on the bars and screaming. Hombre muerto!, he's screaming, Hombre muerto! The DA looks at me and asks, What's he saying? Dead man, I tell him. He says dead man.

The DA walks me back downstairs to the desk and shakes my hand. Thank you, Mrs. Medina, he says.

I tell him, Look, don't call me Mrs. Medina no more, okay? They're going to check and find out anyway and it doesn't make any difference. It's not Mrs. Medina, I tell him. It's Dulcie Gomez. I'm only married in my mind.

I got what I wanted, I guess. Chuey's lawyer—this woman

from the Public Defender's office—and Chuey's mom, and me, we all worked on Chuey. We worked on him real good. Chuey testified against Sleepy Chavez.

The DA wouldn't make any deals. The brother that was on the critical list recovered, but he never came to court. He hadn't seen nothing, and they didn't need him anyway. They done this test that showed that Sleepy had fired a gun and then they found the gun. Some tow truck driver brought it in. It was under a car he towed away. Sleepy's fingerprints was all over it. The only thing the DA said he would do, if Chuey testified, was talk to the judge when it was time for the sentencing. Ms. Bernstein, Chuey's lawyer, said it was probably as good a deal as we could get.

Chuey had to stand trial next to Sleepy. Every day Sleepy blew him kisses and told him he was a pussy and a maricon. Ms. Bernstein never complained about it. She said it might help with the jury.

I was surprised at the judge. I didn't think she would let that stuff go on. Every day Sleepy did something stupid. There was all this yelling and pointing, and she never said nothing. The judge was this black chick about forty. She wore a different wig and different nails every day. She sat there playing with her wooden hammer. It didn't seem like she was listening. If you ask me, she was losing it. She called a recess once when one of her nails broke. Ms. Bernstein was real polite to her. She said this was the best judge we could get because she was known for her light sentences.

Ms. Bernstein didn't even try to prove that Chuey was innocent. All she did was show that he didn't know what he was doing. She said he was stoned that day, and she said he was easily led. Even Chuey's mom got up and said that Chuey was easily led, from when he was a little boy.

It was weird to watch. They talked about him like he wasn't there. Ms. Bernstein would show that Chuey was a fool, and then Sleepy's lawyer would try to show that Chuey wasn't a fool. He couldn't do it. Everybody in the courtroom thought Chuey was a fool by the time they got done. Chuey sat at that table listening, and he got smaller and smaller, while Sleepy Chavez kept showing off for all the vatos locos and got bigger and bigger.

The jury said that Sleepy was guilty, but they couldn't make their minds up about Chuey. They didn't think he was innocent, but they didn't think he was guilty, either. They didn't know what to do. The judge talked to them some more, and they came back in ten minutes and said Chuey was guilty but with like mitigating circumstances.

The DA did stand up for Chuey when it came to the sentencing. The judge sent Sleepy Chavez to the California Youth Authority, until he turned twenty-one, and then after that he had to go to prison. The judge said she wanted to give Sleepy a life sentence, but she couldn't because of his age. She gave Chuey probation and time served.

The courtroom went crazy. All the gangs from Shaky Town were there. 42nd Flats, the Avenues and even some from White Fence. They all start booing the judge, who finally bangs her hammer. Sleepy stands up. He makes a fist over his head and yells, Flats! La Raza Unida, and they go crazy some more.

I couldn't believe it. Sleepy Chavez standing there with both arms in the air, yelling Viva! like he just won something, and Chuey sits there with his head down like he was the one going to prison.

I go down to kiss Chuey, and Sleepy spits at my feet. Hey, puta, he tells me, take your sissy home.

I can't stand it. I tell him, Sleepy, those guys in prison are gonna fuck you in the ass and I'm glad.

Sleepy says, Bullshit. I'll be in the Mexican Mafia before I get out of C.Y.A. I'll tell you who gets fucked in the ass, puta, your sissy, li'l Chuey. He yells at Chuey, Hey, maricon. Hombre muerto. Chuey don't never raise his head.

I talked to the DA afterward. I said, You saw those guys. Chuey needs help. He helped you, you should help him. What about those relocation programs? The DA could give a shit. He cares for Chuey about as much as Sleepy Chavez. He just packs his briefcase and walks away, shaking hands with everybody. The TV is waiting for him outside.

Ms. Bernstein says she'll see what she can do about police protection. I tell her that ain't going to make it. The only thing that will make it is if Chuey gets out of East LA. She says there's nothing to keep Chuey from moving, as long as he tells his probation officer and keeps his appointments. She doesn't understand. The only way Chuey will move is if they make him. She says they can't do that.

I tried to make him move. I tell him, Chuey, they going to kill you. Sooner or later. He doesn't want to talk about it. All he'll say is, Forget it. Flats is my home.

The night he got out, Chuey came to my sister's house where I was babysitting. I wanted him so bad. After I put the kids to bed, we made love. He looked so fine, but it wasn't any good. It wasn't like Chuey at all. He hardly would kiss me. It was like I could have been anyone. After we made it, all he wanted to do was drink wine and listen to records. Every time I tried to talk, he got mad.

On the street, the first month after the trial, the cops were doing heavy-duty patrols. It seemed like there was a black-and-white on every corner. They sent the word out through the gang counselors that Shaky Town was going to stay cool or heads would get broken. They busted the warlords from the 42nd Flats and the Avenues for like jay-walking or loitering.

None of the 42nd Flats would talk to Chuey. They cruised his house and gave him cold looks, but there was too many cops to do anything. Chuey went back to work at Raul's Body Shop. Raul said he didn't care about the gang stuff and Chuey was a good worker, but then things started happening. Chuey was getting drunk and stoned every night, and then he started smoking at work, too. Plus windows got broken at the body shop, then there were fires in the trash cans, and over the weekend someone threw battery acid on a bunch of customers' cars. Raul told Chuey he'd have to let him go. He didn't fire Chuey. He just laid him off so Chuey could collect unemployment.

The night that he got laid off, I took him to dinner and a movie, *Rocky* something, I forget the number. I didn't want him to get down. After the movie, I took Chuey to the No-tell Motel in Eagle Rock. It cost me all my tips from two weekends. They had adult movies there and a mirror over the waterbed.

Chuey got into it a little. He'd been smoking weed at the movie, and he was real relaxed. He lasted a long time. It wasn't great for me. I was too worried about what I had to ask, and also he wasn't really there. Maybe because of the weed, but it was like that time when he first got out of jail. I could have been anyone.

When he was done, I turned off the TV and laid down next to him with my head on his chest. We had a cigarette. When I put it out, I kissed his ear and whispered, Chuey, let's get out of Shaky Town. You got a trade, I said. We could move anyplace. We could get married. We could go to San Francisco or San Diego. We could just live together if you want. I don't care. But we got to get out of here.

Chuey sat up. He pushed me down off his chest. Flats is my home, he said. Chuey, I said, they're going to kill you. He looked at me like I was a long way off and then he nodded, and his eyes were just like that DA's. With the numbers. That's right, Chuey said. They're going to kill me. The numbers flamed up in his eyes like a match. You did this to me, bitch.

Chuey, I said, I love you. He said it again, You did this to me, bitch, and after that he wouldn't talk. We didn't even spend the night.

After he got on unemployment, he filled up his day with weed and wine. I seen him walking right on the street with a joint in one hand and a short dog of white port in the other. Chuey's color TV, he calls it. I had to be in school, I couldn't babysit him. On the street, none of his old friends would talk to him and there was no place he could hang out. Even people who didn't know him didn't like him around. White Fence had put out the word that they were going to do him as a favor to 42nd Flats. No one wanted to be near

Chuey in case there was shooting.

When I got out of school every day, I'd go find him. I tried to get him interested in other stuff, like school, so he could get his high school diploma, or a car. I was even going to front him some of the money, but he didn't want it. All he wanted was his weed and his wine. I even set him up for a job with my cousin who's a plumber, but Chuey said no, he said unemployment was enough. He just kept slipping, going down, and I couldn't pull him up. There wasn't nothing I could do.

He started hanging out with the junkies. They were the only ones, except his family and me, that would talk to him. The junkies hang out in this empty lot across from Lupe's Groceries. A Korean guy owns it, but he's afraid to change the name. He's afraid of the junkies, too. They steal him blind and shoot up in his alley. They got some old chairs and a sofa in the lot, and they sit there, even when it rains. It wasn't too long before Chuey started doing reds. If you ask me, reds are the worst pill around. Red freaks are like zombies. They talk all slurred and spill things. The only thing that's good about them is they don't fight too much, like white freaks, and if they do, they don't hurt each other.

It was hard to be around Chuey once he started doing reds. He'd want to kiss me and his mouth was always full of spit, and then he'd try to feel me up right in front of other guys. I hated it, even if they were just junkies.

Then I heard he was doing smack. Chuey didn't tell me, his uncle did. They were missing money from the house and a stereo. They found out Chuey had done it, and they found his kit. The only thing I'd noticed was that he wasn't drinking so much and he was eating a lot of candy bars.

The weird thing was that once he got to be a junkie, the 42nd Flats stopped hassling him so much. Gangs are funny that way. They treat junkies like they was teachers or welfare workers. They don't respect them. It's like a truce or like they're invisible. I don't know now whether they're going to kill him or not. Maybe they think the smack will do it for them or maybe they're just waiting for the cops to go away or maybe they're saving him for Sleepy Chavez's little brother, who gets paroled out of Juvie next month. I don't know. They still come by the junkie lot. We'll be sitting there and a cruiser will pull up with like four or five dudes inside and you'll see the gun on the window. They call him names, Calavera, which is like a skeleton, or they whisper, Muerto, hombre muerto, but it's like they're playing with him. The other junkies think it's funny. They started calling him Muerto Medina. Chuey don't care.

Sometimes I skip sixth period and come down and sit with him. That's the best time of day. He's shot up and mellow by then. I cut out coming by in the morning 'cause he'd be wired and shaky, and if he'd just scored he'd want me to shoot up with him. But by late afternoon, he's cool. It's real peaceful there in the lot. The sun is nice. We sit on the sofa, and I hold his hand. I like to look at him. He's getting skinny. but he's still a pretty dude. Chuey nods and dreams, nods and dreams, and I sit there as long as I can. It's what I can do.

THE GARLIC EATER

MR. KIM SQUATTED in the shadowed storage room of his market, Lupe's Groceries, contemplating his new gun. Beneath the single overhead lamp, the gun lay on a green felt cloth in a pool of light. It was a nickel-plated .38-caliber Smith & Wesson, a snub-nosed revolver, gleaming from its light coat of oil: truncated, obscenely bulky beside Mr. Kim's slim fingers, blue-black against his ivory-colored skin.

This gun, like much in Mr. Kim's present life, was a compromise. He had wanted a Luger. The Luger fit his hand and reminded him of the spy movies of his boyhood, but the salesman at Big Red's Gun Shop in Highland Park would not allow him to buy it. This salesman, a large, florid man with cotton-white hair, who turned out to be Big Red, asked Mr. Kim's reasons for buying a gun and then explained why the Luger was not the gun for him.

"Look, pal," said Big Red, who took the Luger from Mr. Kim's fingers and put it on the glass counter. "Do you want to kill someone?"

Mr. Kim looked at the Luger and at the salesman. His English was not good. He didn't clearly understand the question or what the desired answer might be.

Big Red answered for him, "Of course you don't want to kill someone. What you want is a deterrent. You buy that Luger, pal, you'll have to use it."

Mr. Kim stared fixedly at the Luger, so Big Red continued. "Let me make sure I got my facts straight. You got a grocery store, right? In a bad neighborhood, right?" Mr. Kim nodded yes to the first question and felt he should discuss the second, but the man was still talking. "So who you dealing with there?" Again, he answered his own question: "You got crackheads, right? You got street gorillas, crazies, glue-sniffers, red freaks, junkies. You got kids, right?" He pointed to the Luger. "Pal, those kids don't even know what that is. They think it's a squirt gun. You buy it, you'll use it."

Big Red lifted the .38 from the glass display case and placed it reverently beside the Luger. "Now this," he said. "They know what this is."

Mr. Kim listened to the voice of his daughter. She was calling the prices as she rang up a customer's purchases. The cash drawer opened and closed with the ting of a bell, and then the door warning buzzed as the customer left the store.

He flicked the gun, and the fluted cylinder swung out. Mr. Kim rotated the cylinder. He sighted through each empty chamber at the overhead lamp. Each bore was clean, flawlessly machined and honed. The cylinder rotated easily, with precise clicks at each stop. Mr. Kim loaded each chamber with a cartridge from the box before him. The bullets were a gift from Big Red—hand-loaded brass shells with round-nosed copper-jacketed slugs—"Your basic stopper," he'd called them. Mr. Kim matched the cylinder to the frame with a firm click and held the gun up under the light, admiring the checkered walnut grips and the golden inset buttons with the interwoven S&W. It was, as Big Red had said, American craftsmanship at its finest.

Mr. Kim felt his daughter's eyes upon him. She spoke to him in Korean, "Where will you keep it?" It was respect on her part; her English was excellent. He answered in English, "Build shelf," then corrected himself, "I *will* build shelf. Under the cash register."

"It scares me," she said. "Do we have to have it?"

Mr. Kim spoke in Korean; the emotion was too strong for his English. "What else can I do, Lily? They beat your mother. They beat her like a dog."

Mr. Kim never built the shelf. That first day, while he was planning the shelf, he carried the gun with him in his jacket and became used to its bulk and comfort.

When he took out the trash in the late afternoon, he surprised two junkies in his alley. With his elbow secretly pressed against the gun in his jacket pocket, he advanced to where they crouched, studying an unfolded paper packet. Mr. Kim slammed the trash can down and they broke for the mouth of the alley before they realized who it was. Some of the powder in the packet spilled.

Enraged, they turned back, and Mr. Kim screamed at them, "Police here soon!" They looked at him, in their calculating junkie way, and decided something had changed. The larger of the two went back to the spilled powder, blew it together, and scraped it up with a matchbook. When he had funneled it back into the packet, he stood and pointed at Mr. Kim. "Your ass! Buckwheat!"

Mr. Kim's hand was still outside his jacket, but he clutched the gun and stood his ground, waiting until they crossed the street to the empty lot where the junkies hung out.

For Mr. Kim it was a moment, the first time since he'd leased the grocery that he had gained respect. Standing there in the alley, he dedicated the moment to his wife. Sun May had been in the hospital now a week. They had wired her broken jaw, bound her bruised ribs. Her soul would take longer to heal. She still refused to look at Mr. Kim when he came for his nightly visit.

Awake and dreaming, Mr. Kim was visited by the memory of what had happened. He had been in the storeroom. It was only the buzzer, going on and on, that had drawn him to the front. He heard the buzzer before Sun May's screams. A skinny Mexican man wearing a hooded sweatshirt was trapped in the doorway. He had a packaged pound cake under his left arm and a quart bottle of Night Train in that hand. Sun May was clutching his knees. Her head was down, pressed against the man's thighs, and she screamed each time his fist smashed against her head or bent neck, but she wouldn't let go.

The man dropped the pound cake as he shifted the wine bottle to his right hand. He beat her with the heavy bottle until she slid down his legs. Her face turned upward as her grip loosened, and it was then that her jaw was broken; the bottle smashed against her jawbone with a crack, and the orange wine shot into the air as she was driven to the floor.

The Mexican stepped out of the loose circle of her arms and kicked her in the ribs. Mr. Kim, who had frozen in the storeroom doorway a few seconds earlier, charged out shouting. The man held the broken bottle out in front of him, slashing the air, and backed out the door.

Mr. Kim could never recall the face. He remembered the jagged teeth of the bottle, the glassy chemical eyes shrouded by the hood of the sweatshirt, and then the man turned and ran off down the street, veed elbows pumping, the soles of his shoes flashing. The buzzer droned on and on until Mr. Kim could drag his wife clear of the doorway and the door clicked shut.

Mr. Kim peered through the door blinds. The two junkies he'd chased out of his alley were telling their story across the street to the other junkies.

The tall one sat on one sofa, talking to the others lounging around him on the broken-up sofas and old armchairs the junkies had hauled to the vacant lot; he was describing with elaborate, accusatory jabs of his forefinger what Mr. Kim had done to him in the alley and—Mr. Kim supposed—what he was going to do to Mr. Kim. The smaller junkie stood behind him, violently nodding his head in outraged agreement; up and down, so strongly sometimes that his eyes closed. "Yeah," Mr. Kim heard him yell. "Yeah. That's right, bro."

The indignation of the junkies, even when they were caught stealing, always surprised Mr. Kim. "So what?" they told him. "Fuck you," they told him. "You're ripping off the people, man." What was just as surprising was that the anger did not last. In an hour that same man out there yelling might be in his store, to buy wine or steal candy.

The discussion across the street had ended. One of the junkies, the dark one that Mr. Kim thought of as the educated junkie, had a liter bottle of Coca-Cola; it was not clear who it belonged to. He was holding the plastic bottle over the head and upstretched arms of the small junkie, teasing him. The rest were yelling, pointing, taking sides. Someone pushed the educated junkie over the back of a sofa. As he toppled, he tossed the bottle to a friend, and the game continued. Except that they were so lazy, the group reminded Mr. Kim of the tame flocks of ducks and cormorants, the long-necked fishing birds of his native coast. It was the same noise, the same squabbling and posturing, the rapid ritual displays of defiance and submission.

Even if he no longer feared the junkies, Mr. Kim still hated them. It was the lack of respect he felt from them. They had been the first to withhold respect, and all the others had followed.

When he had first taken over the store, the junkies had swarmed the place. Anxious to please, reluctant to offend new neighbors, Mr. Kim waited on them patiently, politely deflecting their requests for credit, keeping silent when they tried to haggle over prices.

That first week had been endless and disheartening.

The junkies wandered the store, talking to each other in Spanish, while he and Sun May behind the counter argued in Korean; both sides switched to English to conduct transactions. He remembered the tall junkie holding up a bottle of Thunderbird, saying, "I'll give you a dollar for this. One dollar," while Sun May, nearly in tears, pointed at the price tag and repeated, "Two dollar, eighty-six cent." The junkie kept yelling, as though they couldn't comprehend, "I'll give you a dollar for this wine. One dollar. It ain't even cold."

Mr. Kim's anger flared when he finally understood they were stealing from him. By the end of the first week, they were stealing openly. He told Sun May, "They think we're stupid people. Ignorant." He threw them out; they returned. Finally, he refused to let in more than one of them at a time.

The educated junkie appeared the second week. He was a very dark man, tall and slim with a jutting beard, and Mr. Kim had not realized he was one of the junkies. He was well dressed for the neighborhood, in a blue terrycloth jumpsuit and expensive running shoes. He spoke excellent, musical English, and as he talked his long fingers fluttered and pointed gracefully. In a cultured manner, Mr. Kim had thought then, like the hand movements of tai chi. Alfonso, the man's name was Alfonso, Mr. Kim remembered. He was not a Negro. He came from some country below Mexico—Mr. Kim could not remember which—and he had spent time in Okinawa.

Mr. Kim had been alone in the store that morning when the man came to the counter for the first time. He pointed behind Mr. Kim to a small pyramid of jars. "I see," the man said, "you have some kimchi back there." Mr. Kim looked at the jars of pickled cabbage; the bok choy and garlic and peppers floating in bright red juice. "Yes," Mr. Kim said. "Yes! Kimchi. You know kimchi?"

"Sure," the man said, "I had it all the time in Okinawa. Tasty stuff. Very tasty."

The shelves behind Mr. Kim were a display of Korean goods. Two Korean flags, white silk with the Taoist symbol in the center, the red/black, yin/yang circle surrounded by the four hexagrams, flanked the jars of kimchi; there were pyramids of garlic sauce, tiger wine, and ginseng, dry and floating in bottles. It looked like a shrine. Sun May thought it was foolish to put the only goods their customers *wouldn't* steal behind the counter, but Mr. Kim liked the display.

This man was the first to notice any of the Korean products. "Is that kimchi spicy?" he asked Mr. Kim. "I like it hot." Mr. Kim handed him one of the jars and said, "Spicy. Yes. Very spicy." After looking over the relish, the man asked about everything else on the shelves. Ginseng he knew about. He had never seen tiger's wine before. Mr. Kim held the bottle up and swirled it so that the fine white powder in the bottom—the ground tiger bone—floated up into the clear rice wine like dust in a sunbeam. The tiger's bones were to make one brave. Mr. Kim told the man about tigers: their courage, their intelligence, how sensitive and easily insulted they were, which was why it was necessary to apologize to the tiger before drinking his bones.

It was while he was talking about tigers, Mr. Kim realized afterward, that the other two junkies came in the store. He knew the door buzzer might have sounded, but he couldn't remember hearing it. He had been talking happily about tigers and Korea, about the Chinese man in Seoul who had bought and eaten a whole tiger to become fierce, when the junkies had rushed out the door, bent over and bulky from the cans and bottles and packages they had stolen from Mr. Kim's shelves. They ran off up the street, laughing wildly, and Mr. Kim understood. That man had stood at his counter, hands fluttering and pointing, his voice had gotten louder; it was all to screen the stealing.

Alfonso was holding the tiger wine to the light now, jiggling it. "This stuff," he was saying, "is like the worm in the mezcal bottle. You know about mezcal?" he asked Mr. Kim. "Mezcal makes you brave because it makes you crazy."

Mr. Kim looked at him sadly and took the bottle back. "Go with your friends," Mr. Kim told him.

Alfonso looked him over. The smile was gone; the contempt that had been behind the smile showed plainly. The man reacted as though he'd been insulted. He picked up the jar of kimchi and opened it. The pungent odor filled the store. He held the jar up to his nose and jerked his head away with a look of disgust. "Whoo," he said. "What you trying to sell me? This is junk kimchi, hombre. Number ten. You understand what I'm telling you? Number ten." The man put the open jar down on the counter and walked out. Mr. Kim never protested. He felt deeply shamed; the words wounded him more because the man was not ignorant.

When Alfonso came into the store after that, he was always insulting. One lunchtime, when Sun May was making noodles in the back, the man walked in, sniffed, and said loudly, "Garlic heads! Fish-head stew with garlic. That's what you like, right? That's the trouble with Korea. Too much garlic. The Japanese knew, didn't they? They never say Koreans, do they? They call you Garlic Eaters." He called Mr. Kim Garlic Head, he called Sun May Garlica, and Lily, Garlic Girl.

The disrespect of the junkies had led, Mr. Kim felt, to the disrespect of others. The children stole; the parents complained of his prices. He took down the flags, put the tiger's wine, kimchi, ginseng, and garlic sauce in the storeroom. He called the painter and canceled his order; the sign would stay the same: Lupe's Groceries, not Kim's Store.

In the evening, when Mr. Kim took the trash out again, he looked across the street at the junkies, sitting on their sofas before a small fire. None of them had returned to his alley that day. The ones who had come in the store had been wary. Mr. Kim lifted the trash can overhead and shook the trash into the dumpster. As he lifted the can, the gun bumped against his ribs. He thought again, as he had each time the gun touched his side or he felt its bulk through the cloth, perhaps things could change.

Mr. Kim was arranging cut flowers in the front window when he saw Mrs. Espinosa coming down the hill on her canes. If he had made a friend in the neighborhood, it was the widow Espinosa, and it was because of the flowers.

From the day he'd taken over the store, he had stocked the front window with cut flowers: carnations, daisies, mums, gladiolas. The hardier flowers, those that could survive without refrigeration.

Mr. Kim sold them for only a little more than his cost. He enjoyed his early-morning stop at the wholesale flower market, and the flowers there were cheap, particularly because he was willing to take short lots and culls. The flowers were the one thing in his present life that reminded him of home. His mother had been a wonderful gardener and also taught flower arranging. No civic function or temple ceremony in their village was complete without one of his mother's spare, artful arrangements. Mr. Kim had her skill in his hands, but his gardening was confined to window boxes and planter boxes in front of the store.

Mrs. Espinosa was also a gardener, but arthritis and an increasingly bad back limited the range of her garden. Mr. Kim had been to see it. She had banks of calendulas, poppies and gazanias, and geraniums in pots. The rest of the plot was vegetables: fava beans, chayote and summer squash, tomatoes, peppers, and a fine stand of corn with two marijuana plants hidden in the middle of the second row. Mrs. Espinosa was not at all embarrassed by these plants. She followed a family tradition: Her mother and her grandmother had both brewed marijuana as a tea. Now that she had arthritis, she brewed her own marijuana and yerba buena, and the tea helped with the pain. The cornstalks were to hide the plants from the kids in the neighborhood, not from the police.

Mrs. Espinosa made a daily trip to the grocery for her small needs, mainly cat food, milk, and something sweet for her dessert, and then she would pick out her flowers. Mr. Kim made an arrangement for her and kept them aside; she would add to it from other bouquets.

Occasionally she brought seedlings to him. The blowsy purple cosmos in the semishaded box were hers, so were the trim vinca plants in the sun. She had brought a potted geranium for Sun May when they took her to the hospital and also a small bag of marijuana, which she tried to make Mr. Kim take to her. He knew it probably was a better pain-killer, as Mrs. Espinosa said, than anything the hospital could provide, but the idea of carrying it terrified him.

Mr. Kim opened the door and held it open as Mrs. Espinosa approached; the droning buzzer made him think of Sun May. Mrs. Espinosa shuffled forward, a walnut-colored, bent old woman, wearing her unvarying black dress and black mantilla and an Esprit shopping bag on her arm. Once inside, he guided her to a chair near the counter, sat her down, and waited for her to regain her breath.

"Something special today," Mr. Kim said. He brought out two pots and put them on the counter. "One for Sun May, one for you." Both plants were in vigorous bloom with orange trumpet-shaped flowers, freckled with black spots, as delicate as the first speckles on a banana.

Mrs. Espinosa reached to touch a petal. "Ahh," she said. "Lirio. Azucena."

"Tiger lily," Mr. Kim said. "Na-ri. First grown in Korea. There is a story." Mr. Kim couldn't say that Mrs. Espinosa always understood what he said, but she always listened. Her sturdy fingers tested the lily's stalk, then rubbed a glossy leaf.

"In Korea," Mr. Kim said, "old, old days, a hermit pulled an arrow from a tiger's paw and they became friends. When tiger die, he asked the hermit for magic, to keep him around, so his body become the tiger lily. When hermit die, drowned you know, tiger lily looks for him everywhere, spreads all over the world."

"How much?" Mrs. Espinosa said. She rubbed her thumb and forefinger together.

"De nada," Mr. Kim said; it was the only Spanish besides "Migra," the neighborhood term for the Immigration Service, that he could pronounce. "A present." She nodded.

"One other thing," Mr. Kim said. "Very special." He went to the window and returned, holding a long-stemmed pink carnation. He held it up for her to see. "One stalk," he said. "Three flowers." The long stem had a flower on top and two below, all equal and perfectly formed. "In Korea," Mr. Kim said, "they use flowers like these for..." He couldn't think of the English. In Korean it was *ye-on*. "For fortune-telling." It was as close as he could come. "You tie in your hair. If the bottom flower dries first, misfortune in youth. Middle flower, middle life. If the top flower dries first, old age will be difficult. My mother showed me this when I was a boy."

"What if they all dry at once?" Mrs. Espinosa asked.

"Ahh," Mr. Kim said. "Sad life."

He handed the flower to Mrs. Espinosa. She turned it, looking at each pink fluffy bloom, and then set it firmly on the counter. "No," she said. "No. You keep it. At my age, I don't want to know."

In the afternoon, while Lily was still in school, an emissary from his wife's family, her uncle, Joong Sook, came. Joong knocked on the front door of the store, as though it were a house, and waited for Mr. Kim to open it. Years before, in Seoul, when Mr. Kim could no longer endure Sun May's family walking into his house unannounced, he had finally asked that they telephone first, or at least knock.

Since then, with ostentatious civility, her family knocked—all but her mother, who refused to knock but would not enter without an invitation. Once she had stood in their screen porch for several hours, until Lily had noticed she was there—the rest of Sun May's family now knocked, and they also told anyone who listened that they were not welcome.

Mr. Kim opened the door. Joong was an officious, energetic man of fifty—bald, moon-faced, muscular in his T-shirt and painter's pants. He wasted no time. "Sun May has left the hospital," he told Mr. Kim. "She wanted to go home."

Home, Mr. Kim understood, meant Korea. Seoul, where most of her family still lived.

"Where is she?" Mr. Kim asked.

Joong let his triumph show. "On the plane," he said. "Home tomorrow."

Mr. Kim knew it was true, and he found he was not surprised. Sun May had hated Los Angeles, the heat and the coarseness of their neighbors. She had refused to look at him since the beating. He'd thought at first it was because she was ashamed of her swollen face, wired mouth, and bruises. It wasn't that. She didn't want to look at *him*, not the other way round. Her family, of course, would be glad to help her in her flight. Joong was waiting for some response from him. Nearly anything, Mr. Kim knew, would add to Joong's satisfaction.

He thought suddenly of Lily. He wondered if she had known, if she had talked with her mother. Mr. Kim thought back. All that week he had looked up to find Lily watching him; when she was caught, her head would drop. Like her mother, she did not want him to see what was in her eyes. He understood then that mother and daughter had talked, and Lily had made her choice. She'd chosen to stay, which meant she could not tell her mother's secret. She could only watch him, knowing the pain and shame he would soon feel. His heart went out to her.

Joong was still waiting. When it was clear Mr. Kim would stay silent, Joong spoke. "Here!" he said. His hand thrust in the general direction of the neighborhood and then more specifically, pointing at the counters and shelves of the small store. "She did not feel you could protect her here," Joong said.

Mr. Kim considered telling Joong about his gun, about the difference it had already made. He stood with his hand in his jacket pocket, his thumb rubbing the barrel, and knew it would make no difference to Joong. It would only provide delicious gossip at the next family gathering.

Nothing could change the way they thought of him: the weakling. The reserved and accepting Buddhist in that family of bustling Methodists.

Again, Joong waited. Mr. Kim did not speak. Joong left, pulling the door shut behind him with a bang.

It was late afternoon. Lily was not back from school, but she would be soon and Mr. Kim still could not decide what to say to her.

After Joong had left, Mr. Kim had locked the door and ignored the customers who had banged on it while he tried to think. He could not think.

Now Alfonso, the educated junkie, was out there,

banging on the glass, rattling the blinds, and it seemed pointless not to let him in. He could at least be making money; Sun May's family would approve.

Mr. Kim slipped the lock, and Alfonso reeled into the store. The man was high, or drunk, or both. "Mr. Garlic Head," Alfonso said. "A little wine. I need a little wine to keep it going." Mr. Kim said nothing, only watched him go to the cooler and pull out a bottle of Night Train. He turned with the bottle in his fist and scanned Mr. Kim, in that calculating junkie way, and Mr. Kim could see what registered in his eyes: Something had gone wrong in the garlic eater's life. Something that might be to his advantage.

Alfonso walked toward the door, waving a hand gracefully. "Pay you Tuesday." Mr. Kim fired through the cloth of his jacket, without aiming. The roar of the gun was staggering in the small space—Tiger, Mr. Kim thought, Tiger—and the man dropped to the floor.

A mistake, Mr. Kim thought. My finger was on the trigger. I shot without thinking, without aiming. No, he decided, not true. I was not thinking, but it was exactly what I meant to do.

Mr. Kim walked over and looked down at the man. The bullet had passed through his side, just above the waist. Alfonso lay there, his teeth bared in silent agony, his body bent in an S: the curve of pain in a fish, bending on itself as the hook is pulled from its mouth, the sine curve dividing the yin from the yang. Mr. Kim stepped over him and locked the door.

On the way back, the man reached for Mr. Kim. His arm stretched out and his fingers touched Mr. Kim's ankle. Mr.

Kim stopped. Alfonso hissed through a rictus of pain, "No Migra. Por favor. No Migra." Mr. Kim looked down at the pleading fingers that touched but dared not curl around his ankle. He came to.

"No Migra," Mr. Kim said.

Mr. Kim bent down and lifted Alfonso's pink sweatshirt. The bullet had passed through cleanly. Behind the counter he found Sun May's white grocer's smock. He tore the cloth, folded it, and slipped it under Alfonso. From his small shelf of medical supplies Mr. Kim opened packets of gauze and cotton batting, doused them with Betadine and pressed them in around the wound, wincing as Alfonso winced, then tied the smock loosely to hold the compress in place.

He thumbed the cap from an aspirin bottle and poured the pills into his palm. He pressed two between Alfonso's lips, followed his eyes, and gave him the rest of the handful. He thought about water to wash them down, but again Alfonso's eyes caught him. They were shifting toward the bottle of wine that had rolled to a stop beside them. Mr. Kim found a Styrofoam cup, poured a half cup of the orange wine, and held it to the man's mouth. He sipped, swallowed, then shifted a little to take some more. Mr. Kim poured another half cup and stood up. The glaze of pain was receding from Alfonso's eyes. Alfonso reached for the cup.

Mr. Kim sat down behind his counter. Soon he would call the ambulance, now he was waiting for Lily's face at the window.

The carnation, with its three freak blooms, was before him. He had been ten when his mother had put the carnation in his hair, plaiting the locks around it. The top blossom had dried first and his mother had been pleased. "First flower," she'd said. "Only the last years of one's life will be difficult." He had not thought they would come so soon.

DOÑA ANITA

THE OLD BORRACHO is playing his guitar again, I can hear him through our hedge. I am sitting on my porch swing as I am sure he is sitting on his in these twin houses. That old borracho, Emiliano Gomez, has lived next door to me for more than forty years and he has been playing his guitar the whole time, but it doesn't sound the way it used to. The hedge is eugenia and has a new bug that shrinks the leaves and fills them with blisters, and it has got very thin so you can hear better, but he also plays differently than before he lost most of the three fingers on his right hand. He always said he was lucky not to lose his chord hand. He strums with the stubs and even picks a little with his thumb and little finger.

Forty years ago, when we were all newly married and there was no hedge, he and my Lorenzo would sit in the yard and serenade me and Josie. My Lorenzo couldn't play anything, but he had a deep voice and he sang like an angel going to heaven. When he sang "Volver," he could make both me and Josefina cry.

We were so happy then and I'm not making this up, I know you can lie to yourself because of course you were happy, you were young, but we really were. There was plenty of work, and a man could earn enough so that his wife could really raise the kids. I was always sorry that Lorenzo and Emiliano didn't work together, they were good friends, but Lorenzo was a paving contractor and Emiliano had a more artistic nature. He could carve beautiful things, statues and chairs and even musical instruments until he went to work at the studios. That ruined him, I think, all that money and they broke everything he made. After his son died, everything changed. He loved that boy, Carlos, and after he died that man changed, and I don't just mean about him losing his fingers and losing his job. You can get another job, you can have another kid. Lorenzo and I lost two. God took Ronald and Cathy and we missed them, but we prayed and we had more kids. Emiliano was different, I think he lost his faith. He was always kind to Josie, but he didn't want any more kids and I know that discouraged her. She got the cancer in her forties, and she died well before her time. A few years after Josie died and all the kids were out of the house, Emiliano planted the hedge between our houses, and about the time you couldn't see over there anymore, he started bringing women home. I don't say they were putas, maybe he was picking them up at that Kelsoe's Roundhouse or Las Quince Letras where he spent so much time. Maybe they weren't paid-for whores, but they all delivered and some of them were noisy, we could hear them. They made my Lorenzo smile and turned him into the devil, too. I got no peace those nights.

Some of those nights, sometimes when those women went home, Emiliano would come out on his porch and play his guitar. He'd play the songs of the Revolution, but he would play them slowly. "The Adelita" is a lively song, but when you play it slowly it is a love song, full of longing. Every time it would take my Lorenzo out to the porch. Play it again, Lorenzo would say through the hedge, and Emiliano would. He'd play it three or four times and sometimes "La Cucaracha," which is a thoughtful and funny song, played slow, and when Emiliano was ready to go to bed, he would play Lorenzo's favorite. Lorenzo was a tough man, the rock we all washed up against, but when Emiliano played "Cuatro Caminos," that would always make my husband cry. He played it at Lorenzo's funeral, and I couldn't stop crying.

Tonight the old borracho has been playing a lot of Pedro Infante. He's drinking, you can tell, you can hear the ice in his glass. I don't know what he drinks now. He and Lorenzo stayed to tequila in the old days, muy tradicional with the lime and salt, no ice for them in those days, but I think they drank less. I never had a taste for it. Sometimes a beer, but I never really liked it. I do have what my abuela and my mama had, good hot tea—yerba buena and the other herb that helps with the arthritis. They tell me if you smoke it, life seems comical, but in tea it only makes you calm.

Now he's playing a paso doble that takes me back to when we all still danced, and it's lively, and when he stops in the middle he catches me, my toe tapping on the porch boards. He's quiet, and then I hear him refill his glass and then he says through the hedge, What would you like to hear, Doña Anita? and I say "The Adelita," and he plays and I push back on the swing and lift my feet.

HUEVOS

THEY MET AT the Tio Taco stand, eight boys, all seniors at St. Patrick's. There was no plan, except to meet. It was Halloween night, they were seniors, *something* should happen.

No one knew of any parties to crash. Frank Sanchez had heard about a dance, but it was in El Monte and he thought you had to wear a costume. They were hanging out at a liquor store parking lot, below the taco stand, hoping for a wino who might buy beer for them, but none had showed.

Bored, antsy, they clustered in shifting groups. Cars cruised by on the shining black street, still wet from an early evening rain. They watched their breath steam in the chill air, their hands jammed into the slash pockets of their jackets. The fragrant odors of fried tortillas and carnitas and the clean, soapy smell of beans drifted down to them. Two of the boys collected money and went up to order food. They talked, ate, jostled, smoked, and spat until the liquor store owner came out and made them move. It was then, the fourth time he'd proposed it, that they took up Kenny Culver's suggestion.

Kenny, a slight, excitable blond boy whose enthusiasm carried little weight with the group, had proposed that they go egging. "We get some eggs," Kenny had said, "we nail some people." Now, as the liquor store owner herded them toward the sidewalk, Kenny made his suggestion again and added the deciding kicker, "We could nail the fucking school first." No one had a better idea.

Jim Wylie, the meekest of the group, after asking the time of everyone there, discovered that he had to be home by nine. They let Wylie walk and divided themselves up to fit two cars.

Kenny found himself in the wrong car. He'd wanted to ride with Frank Sanchez, in Sanchez's Buick Riviera. So did everyone else, and while Kenny was still talking, they piled in. Kenny was left with Cherzniak and Clark, two football players he scarcely knew, and Cherzniak's battered Ford Business Coupe.

Cherzniak followed Sanchez's Buick to Woody's Ranch Market in Eagle Rock to buy eggs. The suspicious checker there watched them pool their money and pile the cartons of eggs on his checkout counter. There were sixteen dozen altogether. The checker paged the manager, seeking an opinion, but the manager never answered. At length, he took their money, bagged the eggs, and stared at them until they were out of the store. In the parking lot, they divided up the eggs on the hood of Sanchez's Buick. Johnny Martinez leaned back against the fender, cupping a pair of eggs against his crotch. "Check out these cojones," Martinez said. "Real huevos. Extra-large. Grade A."

They set out for the school. Cherzniak led, driving through the back streets toward St. Patrick's. Kenny sat in the back seat, the egg cartons at his feet, and handed out the first dozen: four each, one for each hand, one in either jacket pocket. Cherzniak, driving, risked two in his front shirt pockets.

Kenny was watching Clark and Cherzniak. Both had the same burr haircut, the mark of athletes at St. Patrick's; Clark's was patchier, a home cut, Kenny suspected. It matched his raw features: the broken nose, the bristling jaw, the spread ears, the muscular neck sloping to his shoulders. Clark was a linebacker. Cherzniak was bigger and softer, a defensive tackle. It was clear they were close friends. They were talking about Clark's father, and Cherzniak was saying, with some heat, "You oughta tell Jack to go piss up a rope."

"You're right," Clark said. "What can I say? I know you're right." Kenny wished again that he were in the Buick.

They were approaching the high school from the back, driving under the freeway. In the underpass, Cherzniak and Sanchez turned off their lights and parked beside a huge pillar. The seven of them picked their way down the railroad tracks toward the front of the school. Kenny was last; the eggs in the cupped palms ahead of him bobbed luminously in the dark like cartoon teeth. They bunched together as they closed in on the school gates. Sanchez, who was leading, stopped short, sucking in a breath and holding his arms out to stop them.

Kenny saw some movement behind the gates. "Brother

Cyril," Sanchez said. Kenny recognized the stance: a small man in a black cassock with a green sash. His hands were clasped behind his back, and he patrolled the gates at an aggressive tilt. Definitely Cyril, the school's dean of discipline.

They backed down the tracks. When they got close to the underpass, they turned and ran, all except Clark and Cherzniak. They kept their pace slow to the point of cockiness. When Clark and Cherzniak reached the underpass, they turned, and on a count, lofted their eggs. They sailed out in high, elegant arcs.

The five in the tunnel watched, thrilling at the descent. One egg fell short, spattering on the asphalt, the second smacked against the building. Someone yelled, and then they all did, yelling like charging soldiers as they sprinted for the cars.

Sanchez pulled out, Cherzniak followed. Clark was screaming in the car, "One hell of an arm. One hell of an arm." Kenny, facing the back window, was the only one to see Brother Cyril. Cyril had picked up the skirts of his cassock and given chase, sprinting down the parking lot. As they pulled away, spraying dirt, Cyril was halfway up the chain-link fence; his teeth were bared, but no sound escaped him that Kenny could hear.

Something was released in all of them; they went wild. The first stop sign Cherzniak braked for was smeared with eggs. The yolks, white, and bits of shell slid down the red octagonal sign. Clark and Kenny hit it again. Cherzniak lobbed an egg that missed and then burned rubber away from the stop, fishtailing after the glowing red lights of Sanchez's Buick as it sped up the avenue. Even trailing, they could hear whoops and yells inside the Buick.

Cherzniak caught up and passed the Buick on nerve, running a red light that Sanchez had stopped for. Sanchez gave chase and they charged up Eagle Rock Boulevard together, hurling eggs as they went: at signs, parked cars, storefronts, a movie theater marquee. Two eggs smashed against the glass ticket booth. The startled cashier threw up her arms and pitched back against the wall. Then they hit the theater patrons walking away.

They roared up the boulevard, horns blaring, yelling. They splattered some kids in costume waiting obediently at lights with attendant parents, a drunk slumped on a bus bench who snapped upright as the eggs hit his chest. The wailing cries of the trick-or-treaters, outraged shouts from their parents, and confused cursing from the drunk followed them up the boulevard.

Clark got crazier. He was hanging out of the car, holding on to its sun visor, and firing on the move. Each time he threw, he thrust his hand into the back seat, yelling for Kenny to give him another egg.

Near the bowling alley Clark had Cherzniak slow and made a perfect peg, hitting a woman wearing an ankle-length fur coat. The woman seemed to jolt forward as the egg spattered on the brown fur covering her back. Her husband turned, face red with rage, and charged after them. Kenny hit him on the shoulder with an egg, and Cherzniak had to run another red light. The man pounded after the car, punching the air and screaming, then slowed as they pulled away. They watched gleefully as the boys in Sanchez's Buick came parallel and hit the man with two more eggs as he stomped back toward the sidewalk.

Clark started throwing eggs at oncoming cars. He threw across three lanes and hit the windshield of a Mustang, dead center. A block later he smeared the side window of an oncoming BMW and was rewarded with the shriek of locked brakes and squealing tires. Clark screamed at Kenny to keep feeding him eggs.

Sanchez hit the gas to catch them at a stoplight. The boys in the Buick were cheering as they pulled up. "All right, Clark!" "Hell of an arm!"

Kenny was pissed. Clark had kept him so busy passing eggs that he'd scarcely had time to throw any himself. As the Buick slid alongside and he looked at the flushed laughing faces, his irritation increased. Clark leaned in then and said, "Hey. Load me up."

"Get your own," Kenny told him. Kenny crawled out from his own window. He looked across the flat of the roof at the boys in the Buick. Clark joined him, sitting on his windowsill, and placed an open carton of eggs between them.

Kenny understood. He'd been thinking the same thing as he'd sat there, lightly tossing and catching the egg in his right hand, watching the laughing dudes in the Buick. Johnny Martinez, in the Buick's front seat, looked up at them. "Orale pues," Johnny said. "What's next?"

"Oh, anything we want, I guess." Clark's voice was unnaturally musical. His left foot reached out to nudge Cherzniak's shoulder. Clark continued in a sing-song voice, "How about an omelet?" As he finished the question, he and Kenny lobbed their first eggs into the Buick's open windows and reached for more from the carton. Clark and

Kenny broke a half dozen inside the Buick before the boys managed to crank the windows up. They splattered another six on the windows, hood, and sides. Sanchez was yelling. "Hey, hey, hey. Watch the paint. *Pinche* putos. Cabrones!"

Clark and Kenny both hit the windshield, and Sanchez made the mistake of turning on his windshield wipers. The eggs smeared the windshield. Sanchez got out of his Buick with a baseball bat and murder in his eyes.

Cherzniak didn't wait. He shot through the intersection, angling between two crossing cars. Sanchez flung the bat, which hit one of the oncoming cars, cracking a headlight. "Let's get the hell out of Dodge," Clark yelled.

"Where you want to go?" Cherzniak took a left on Colorado. "Why don't we hit Hollywood Boulevard," Kenny suggested. "Supposed to be great on Halloween."

Clark was up for it, Cherzniak didn't care. "I just want to be far away from Sanchez for a while."

They were on Los Feliz, making the turn for Western, when Kenny made another suggestion.

"I'm starving," Kenny said, "Let's go grab a burger and then cruise. Five minutes, okay?"

"I'm not hungry," Clark said. The suggestion seemed to piss Clark off, which was weird, Kenny thought. He asked Cherzniak. Cherzniak admitted he could do with a burger, maybe some fries, but then he looked at Clark. "Maybe we better skip it," he told Kenny. "I haven't got that much money with me."

"I got money," Kenny said. "Don't worry." He dug into his jeans pocket and pulled out a ball of crumpled singles. Cherzniak looked to Clark. Kenny, registering Clark's raised shoulders and rigid features, remembered the brief flash of embarrassment at the Ranch Market, when Cherzniak had paid for Clark's share of the eggs.

"No. Really," Kenny said. "I just got paid."

Clark's voice kept its edge. "I can't pay you back this week."

Kenny shrugged. "Don't worry about it."

They drove down Western Avenue, closer to the weave of searchlights and corolla of neon that marked the heart of Hollywood. Kenny had a thought.

"You know," he told Clark, "I think there's a job coming open where I work." Clark turned around in the front seat. "It's just boxboy," Kenny said. "Weekends. But it's money."

"I've got a job," Clark said bitterly. "I got two jobs. I don't need anymore jobs."

Cherzniak laughed. "That's what you need," he said, "another job. So Jack can raise your rent." Cherzniak told Kenny, "You believe that shit? His old man *charges* him room and board."

"Fucking Jack," Clark said. "Jack the Boss."

"Is that legal?" Kenny said. "I didn't think they could do that when you're a minor. How old are you?"

"Seventeen," Clark said. "As soon as I turn eighteen, I'll be out of there, baby. Aye-dios. All she wrote. I'll be in the fucking Marines the day I turn eighteen."

"You ought to go see a lawyer," Kenny said.

"Oh yeah," Clark said. "Jack would *love* that. He wouldn't kick my ass too hard. Not too much."

"Big Jack," Cherzniak sang. "Jack the Boss. Big Bad Jack."

"I don't give a rat's ass," Clark said. "Six more months, I'm out of there."

Kenny suddenly remembered Clark on his daily rounds of the cafeteria, trying to trade his peanut butter sandwich to anybody, even freshmen, for anything.

They found a McDonald's on Vine, south of Sunset. They sat on the fenders of the Ford in the parking lot to eat their Big Macs and watch the crowd, costumed and plain, streaming toward the boulevard. Clark, still jittery and sure Sanchez would find them, collected all their remaining eggs and set them in an open carton on the Ford's hood.

They were nearly done. Kenny was stuffing Styrofoam containers into the big bag. Cherzniak leaned close to his ear, his voice was an insinuating crawl. "Check it out."

A tiny Black woman was walking toward them. She wore a black satin jacket, a flame-red blouse, a black mini-skirt the width of a handkerchief, and red high-heeled shoes. The shoes were so disproportionate to her size that she nearly toppled as she walked. Her legs were bowed by the strain, her calf and thigh muscles were like small knots on a branch.

She tottered to the car next to them and leaned against it. Her eyes swam, unfocused, with the right eyelid drooping as her head nodded forward. "Whatchu boys doing?"

"Eatin'," Cherzniak said.

"You boys looking for a party?" Her voice was semi-slurred; some words were clear, then the next word would trail off or lurch, like someone pitching forward on a stair.

Kenny looked at Clark and Cherzniak. "You a hooker?" Kenny said.

"Hard to say, baby. Maybe this is a costume. Why? You a cop?"

"Us?" Kenny said. "You gotta be kidding."

Cherzniak leaned into the light. "What's your name?"

"Tish," she said. "What's that?" She pointed a curved crimson nail at the open carton of eggs on the hood.

"Eggs," Clark said.

"They cooked?" Tish asked.

Kenny shook his head.

"They raw?"

Kenny nodded.

"Gimme one."

"Why?" Clark asked.

"Why? What you think? For breakfast."

Clark lifted one from the carton and tossed it to her. His throw was high, but she snagged it near her shoulder and brought it down. Her hands were small, but the nails were so long that she couldn't close her hand; they caged the egg like a red five-pointed star. She stared at the egg. "What you doing with them?"

"Oh," Cherzniak said. "We throw 'em."

"That's crazy," she said. "That's a waste. Why you do that?"

None of them answered. She slipped the egg into her jacket pocket and pushed off from the car she was leaning against. "That's crazy." One red shoe slid forward until her hips cocked. "You boys got *any* money?" Again, none of them answered. "What a junk night," she said. "Nothin' but kids and cops." She addressed Clark, "Ten bucks. For ten bucks you can get you a hand job."

Cherzniak said, "Will you be here tomorrow?"

She raised a hand and waggled her fingers at them. "Bye."

They watched her wobble off across the lot, pitching, scuffing her shoes. At a seam in the pavement she nearly tripped. "Shit." She stepped out of the shoes and padded away with them slung from her hand; without the high heels, her legs lost all definition. From the back she looked like a child. In front of the restaurant she took the egg out of her pocket and tossed it into the street.

They drove west, all the way to La Brea, and then crossed over to Hollywood Boulevard. They joined the stalled traffic there, near the Chinese Theatre, where a bank of searchlight shafts quivered and reeled in the darkness over the rooftops, signaling the premiere of another *Friday the 13th* sequel. Lines of motionless cars, bumper to bumper, stretched down the boulevard; drivers and passengers had gotten out of some of the cars and were standing on the roofs and fenders.

The sidewalks were thronged with the costumed, carousers, tourists, Latino families, and street people. "Hollyweird," Kenny said. Mounted police bobbed ahead of them at an intersection.

Beside them, a lowered, root beer brown Toyota truck with flashing blue lights in the fender wells and undercarriage was pumping out salsa music at a head-pounding volume. They couldn't see inside the truck; the windows and windshield had been blackened. The noise from competing stereos and exhausts was deafening. The movement of color and light was manic: a continual wash of neon and strobe lamps. There was a blimp overhead showing cartoons. There were searchlights, flashing advertisements, a constant carnival flare of brake lights ahead of them and headlights coming toward them.

They were stopped a long time in front of a bar called Life After Bruce. Two bearded men in drag, the bristles of their beards poking obscenely through putty-colored makeup, leaned against each other in the doorway of the bar, pointing out costumes and shouting comments. "*This*," the one wearing a red sequined gown shouted, "is the best I've ever seen it on the boulevard." His companion squeezed his shoulder delightedly. "This is our night, Roy," he yelled. "This is the Holy Night of Nights."

A man walked by wearing a tuxedo and orange blinders. An enormous hairy foot protruded from his mouth. A mummy trailing ten feet of gray tatters pushed an empty stroller. Four shirtless teenaged boys, whose only costume seemed to be fake blood and scar makeup, made their way easily through the crowd chanting in unison: "I've got AIDS. I've got AIDS." The crowd split ahead of them like dirt before a plow. A pregnant nun on roller skates rolled along in their wake, like a car trailing a sirening ambulance.

Near Las Palmas they witnessed a confrontation. A small Mexican evangelist had taken over a crosswalk. He held up an open bible; the shopping cart beside him contained leaflets, books, painted plaster statues of Jesus, Mary, and Joseph, and a tape deck playing hymns. The evangelist was facing a devil in full regalia. The devil had a real mustache and a glued-on goatee. His red satin suit had a peaked cap and a stiff pointed arrow tail that curved to nearly touch his thigh. The evangelist held up his bible. The devil shrieked and shook his pitchfork. The evangelist turned to include the crowd, making the devil his show-piece, and bawled out, "He's not the real devil." He turned back to address the devil directly, "You got a bad condition of the heart." The devil growled and shook his pitchfork again before stomping to the curb, his tail bobbing. "Nobody is perfect!" the evangelist yelled. "Everybody needs Jesus!"

Only Clark was not enjoying himself. He played with the radio, drummed his fingers on the dashboard, and ignored what was going on outside his window.

An older Lincoln with a load of cheerleaders pulled into the lane next to them. Their red-and-white pom-poms filled the rear window shelf and the space between the two girls in the back seat.

Clark came to life. "Move up. Pull up," he told Cherzniak. Cherzniak eased the Ford forward about five feet, until it was right on the bumper of the car ahead and even with the rear door of the Lincoln. Clark leaned out and knocked on the rear window of the Lincoln. A startled pretty face, a dark-eyed girl with a brown shag, turned toward him, and then her window dropped down halfway. "Are those your costumes?" Clark asked.

"What?" she said. "No. We're real cheerleaders." Kenny laughed. "We just left the game," she said.

"Where do you go?" Clark asked.

"Sacred Heart Academy."

"That's what I thought," Clark said. "Did you win?"

She looked at him. "What? Oh." She turned to her

friends, "Did we win?" and turned back laughing. "Yeah, we won. Forty-two to thirty-eight."

The other girl in the back seat leaned forward and looked over the Ford, Clark, and Kenny; she sank back in the seat.

The girl Clark was talking to turned away suddenly, intent on something in the front seat. "Ooh," she said. "Turn that up. Turn that up." The driver twisted the volume knob and an old Go-Go's hit, "Vacation," blasted out. She closed her eyes, with a pleased smile, and danced in place, her small fists shimmying above her shoulders.

Clark was unable to restart the conversation. The Lincoln moved ahead. Clark kept bugging Cherzniak to catch up, but it was impossible. Their lane was locked solid.

A sleek white Thunderbird, a classic from the sixties, was just ahead of the Lincoln. There were four guys in the T-Bird. The two in the back seat were turned around; one waved to the cheerleaders. The cheerleaders were talking animatedly, but their eyes were on the T-Bird.

"Get close to them," Clark told Cherzniak. The two guys who had been staring got out of the T-Bird. They both rolled their shoulders and adjusted their jackets, like athletes getting out of a bus, and walked back to the Lincoln. They were large, one dark haired, one blond; the blond one wore a USC jacket, the dark-haired one wore a maroon blazer with a fraternity crest. Both had exceptional tans. The blond leaned down to the driver's window, the guy in the maroon jacket spoke to the girl on the passenger side. "Give it up, Clark," Kenny said. "Those guys are in college. They're fraternity boys." As the traffic crept forward, the two guys from the T-Bird walked alongside the Lincoln.

"I don't give a rat's ass," Clark said. He leaned out, trying to regain the dark-haired girl's attention. Kenny's voice was mocking: "Give it *up*."

Clark didn't give up. He stretched out farther and farther, calling to her. She was intent on the boy in the maroon blazer. Clark threw a gum wrapper at her door. Then a cigarette butt, then another. Then a handful of cigarette butts, thrown as hard as he could. She never looked Clark's way. The only one who noticed Clark at all was the guy in the maroon jacket, who glanced at them when a butt bounced off his tan loafers. Kenny was suddenly afraid Clark might throw an egg.

The car in front of them pulled ahead. Cherzniak took his foot off the brake; the Ford crept forward. Clark reached over and grabbed the steering wheel; he jerked it toward him so the Ford veered toward the T-Bird and the Lincoln. Kenny leaned over the front seat. Clark had an egg in his other hand. "Don't do it," Kenny said. "Don't do it, you fucker. Those guys would kill us."

The guy in the maroon jacket straightened up. The Ford had stopped with the bumper a foot from his knees. All the girls in the Lincoln were staring at Clark. The other two guys were getting out of the T-Bird. "Oh shit," Kenny said. "Oh shit."

Clark addressed the guy in the maroon jacket: "I'm trying to talk to that girl." Kenny saw, with some relief, that Cherzniak had his hand clamped on Clark's wrist. The guy in the jacket leaned down to the girl with the shag haircut. His voice was deep and assured and amiable. "Did you wish to speak to this gentleman?"

She shook her head. The other girl in the back seat leaned forward and looking directly at Clark said, "Hell, no!"

There was a small pop. Kenny, looking over the seat, saw the yolk and white dripping onto Clark's pants from between his clenched fingers. Cherzniak still held his wrist.

Maroon jacket turned away. The blond leaned down and whispered something to the red-haired girl driving the Lincoln. His fingertips touched her hand on the steering wheel. She smiled, listening to him, and she looked at her friends in the rearview mirror.

The fraternity boys climbed back in the T-Bird. The car pulled out of line and onto a side street. The Lincoln followed them. Kenny watched its winking red turn signal until it rounded a corner and disappeared.

Clark wiped his hands on the seat. "Let's get out of here," he said. Cherzniak pulled out of line, squeezing between two cars whose drivers honked furiously at him. They headed toward Sunset Boulevard.

At the corner of Ivar and Sunset, two men waited for the light, arm in arm, a Dracula with blue eye shadow and a muscular Alice in Wonderland. Clark hit Alice with two eggs, one in the chest, one in his blond wig. Alice yelled, "You bastard" at Clark, and Dracula advanced toward the Ford.

Clark reached under the seat. Kenny heard his fingers scrabbling. Clark got out of the car holding up a tire iron. Dracula hesitated. "Come on, Butt Boy," Clark cooed. He smacked the heavy end of the iron in his palm.

Alice yelled, "Get out of the street, Ron. Now!" Dracula backed away. Clark smashed the iron against the side of the car and then at the pavement, striking sparks. *"Come on."* He held the iron before his eyes, and his voice was hoarse and almost pleading, "Come on. Come on, faggot. Here's something you can suck."

Cherzniak and Kenny dragged him back in the car. The light changed. Cherzniak hit the gas, smoking the tires. Something thumped against the trunk and Alice shouted, "Asshole breeder!" Cherzniak shot down Sunset.

Clark tapped the iron against the metal dash. His eyes were closed, his head bobbed and jerked to some song of his own. Cherzniak went onto side streets, speeding up to fifty, slamming across bumps and dips. It seemed to calm Clark down. By the time they reached the Hyperion bridge, he was sitting up straight and holding the tire iron still.

Cherzniak pulled a U-turn off the Hyperion bridge and drove onto the Glendale Avenue bridge that crossed the LA River and the Golden State Freeway. He slowed and looked over at Clark, checking him. As the car slowed, Clark stared out the windshield at something ahead of them on the roadway. "Hey," Clark said, "pull over." Cherzniak slowed some more. "Stop, goddamnit."

Clark jumped out of the car while it was still rolling. He sprinted into the beams of their headlights, holding up the iron. In a single fluid motion, he brought the iron across his body and flung it. They watched the iron spin, crossing on itself for fifty or sixty feet in the headlights. It went into the dark where it thumped against something scuttling along the bridge wall.

They ran after Clark. He'd retrieved the tire iron by the time they reached him; he was holding it out like a stick, poking at something. A huge brown rat lay on its side next to the bridge wall, its back legs twitched feebly, then were still.

"Jesus," Cherzniak said, "that was a hell of a shot."

"Is it dead?" Kenny said.

Clark poked the rat's stomach, but there was no response. "I don't know," Clark said, "but I'm gonna find out." He looked at Cherzniak. "Get me the flares."

Cherzniak went back to the car while Kenny and Clark stood over the rat. Cherzniak dropped the box on the pavement, struck one of the flares, and handed it to Clark. "Okay, rat," Clark said, "let's see if you're faking." He touched the sputtering flare to the rat's foot-long tail, then moved the flame in, playing it over the rat's puckered anus and below, around the fur-covered balls.

Kenny straightened up. He looked out over the bridge railing and down, into the pit of the freeway where taillights and headlights streamed by. He was ready to go home.

Cherzniak pushed the tire iron down on the rat's chest while Clark twisted the rat's mouth open, forcing the flare into the jaws and then shoving it into the throat. The rat's belly lit up with a red glow. Lice and fleas streamed across the belly fur, moving away from the heat. Red smoke poured from the rat's mouth.

Using the flare like a handle, Clark lifted the rat up and set it on the bridge wall. He lit two more flares and put them on either side of the rat, like candles.

They stood there in the roiling red smoke, watching the flares sputter and burn. The rat's swelling belly glowed like a jack-o'-lantern. "I hate those fuckers," Clark said. "God, I hate those fuckers." The acrid smoke coiled around them.

A stench like burning hair made Kenny's stomach do a slow turn. A smoking black spot appeared on the rat's red belly and grew, like a pupil dilating, and Clark said again, in the same flat, hopeless voice, "I hate those fuckers. I hate them."

EMILIANO PART II: A CURSE ON CHAVEZ RAVINE

I'M READING THE newspaper today, and I see that Peter O'Malley wants to build a new football stadium next to Dodger Stadium. Some of the neighbors are upset. ¡Que surprise! Some of them have been upset since the first O'Malley built the first stadium.

That one was Walter. A big, smart, mean Irishman from Brooklyn. Muy duro. Always with a cigar Cubano. He had a full set of cojones, and he always got what he wanted. Ask Brooklyn, they're not over it yet. A good Catholic, of course. He made sure the Cardinal got good seats. The son, they say, is not so smart and not so mean. He doesn't have to be. We live in a time when if you're tall and not too ugly and you have money, people think you must be smart.

Peter O'Malley will get what he wants. People are scared. All you have to say are the magic words—jobs, taxes, money for the community. Also, he won't have to fight my Aunt Lupe this time around.

People still know the words *Chavez Ravine*, but only the

viejos and viejas really know what that place was. Chavez Ravine, in the '50s, was like living in the hill country of Mexico. No paved streets, no sewers, no electricity, the water came from wells. The first thing you noticed was the scent. It smelled like Mexico. Woodsmoke, chiles, goat shit, tortillas, and beans. Roosters woke you in the morning, but you could see City Hall. The biggest building in town. Huge. Towering over that flat city. People kept pigs, chickens, goats, and cows. I got my first drink of fresh milk and my first horseback ride in Los Angeles in Chavez Ravine.

There were three small barrios—neighborhoods—in the ravine. They all had names. There was La Loma, The Hill. There was Bishop. And there was Palo Verde, Green Tree, where my Aunt Lupe lived.

My Aunt Lupe, also known as La Sinverguenza—that's three words, La Sin Verguenza—The Shameless One. Without shame. Sin means without. Strange, no? But you know it if you order a drink in Mexico. They ask you, *Sin gas* or *Con gas*. Carbonated or not. Lupe was my mother's youngest sister. She was one of the fierce women that Zacatecas is famous for. If she had been born at the turn of the century, she would have been a revolutionary, one of the soldadas. In her place and time, she was a bartender at La Estrella del Norte. Don't think that was a small job. That was the mistake the judge made. Maybe it was a small job, but Aunt Lupe wasn't, and her influence extended well beyond that little bar. She had three husbands, innumerable novios. All of them talked about her wistfully and with respect and perhaps with a little fear, both before and after she died. She had no sons, which I liked as the favorite nephew, and she lived in Chavez Ravine for thirty years.

The official description of Chavez Ravine was a little different from what I knew. Aunt Lupe knew it by heart, and she said it so often that I know it, too. I can't say it the way she said it, flamenco and with iron, but this was what the tax assessor said: *Wasteland. Three hundred acres of scrub. Eroded gullies, gulches, and low hills. Some ramshackle dwellings. None have been on the tax rolls for more than twenty years.*

All the city fathers agreed that a baseball stadium was a good use for wasted land. Earlier they had decided that public housing should be built in Chavez Ravine, but the Red Scare had stalled that. Everyone agreed that giving free land to a rich man was a much better idea. It's only socialism when there are poor people involved. When you give things to rich people, they call it an investment.

When the news came from the city that the remaining residents of Chavez Ravine, Los Holdouts, would have to move—notified by the first letters anyone had gotten for years except at the Post Office—Lupe held meetings. Some people thought they would get money for their houses, but the city said it already owned them, for back taxes. No one could agree what to do. Lupe said they should picket, at the mayor's house, but that was two bus rides away, so she was the only one who did it. Some people picketed in Chavez Ravine, but nobody came to see them. Finally, Lupe threw up her hands and went to court. I don't know how she did it, but she got a hearing. I think they just wanted her to go away. She was bothering all the clerks and the judges at the courthouse, so they gave her the hearing. Aunt Lupe was babysitting me, so I got to go. My mom would have been upset if she knew, but I wasn't going to tell her.

The judge was a very small man with white hair and shaky hands. He dropped his gavel when he was coming in. It was a surprise when he got behind his desk. It was about eight feet off the floor, with a marble wall behind him and the state seal of California, and lights shining down on him and his black robe. He suddenly looked dignified. A big sheriff said, All rise. Everybody else had to stand up, and the judge sat down. The judge put his glasses on and read some papers, and then he looked down at my Aunt Lupe. The first thing he said was that the city owned the land and that she had no standing in court. Aunt Lupe told him he was wrong. She said she was standing and he was the one who was sitting, which she thought was not respectful, and that this was her house and she had lived in it for thirty years and the court didn't have jurisdiction anyway. The judge said, What? and Aunt Lupe brought out a big parchment paper from her purse and handed it up to him. It turned out to be a copy of the original land grant, I think it was to one of the Verdugos. Aunt Lupe had copied it out of a book at the library. The judge said, What is this? and Aunt Lupe said it was a copy of the original land grant because she wasn't going to trust him with the original and that he had no jurisdiction, only the Royal Court of Spain or the Mexican government could decide and she wanted a change of venue. She liked those words, she said them about three times. The judge got mad and pounded his gavel. He said her case was unsupported by fact. She said it was and that because he was supported by her tax dollars, he had to listen. He said, I don't have to listen to this, and then he said, Sit down, Miss Gomez, or I will find you in contempt of court. She kept standing and then she said, It's Mrs. Gomez, and you got another thing wrong. She said she had extreme contempt for the court.

That was pretty much where they left it. The judge ran back to his chambers and called for his bailiff. Two of the guards walked Aunt Lupe outside, and they wouldn't let her back in the building.

When the bulldozers came, Aunt Lupe chained herself to her front door. The bulldozers knocked down the back of her house while she screamed at the foreman. When they'd knocked down most of it, they stopped. Four big guys came and took the door off the hinges. They carried her away on the door, put her in the shade of a cypress tree her father had planted, and then knocked down the rest of the house. Then they cut the chains with bolt cutters and let her go. Then they cut down the tree.

Aunt Lupe died four years after that. Some of the neighbors said she died of a broken heart, but that wasn't true. It was the cancer. Well, quién sabe? It might be a little true. Who is to say how cancer worms its way in. It seems to have more luck with a bruised heart.

When she knew she was dying, Aunt Lupe decided she would put a curse on Chavez Ravine. She talked to a curandera—a doctor or specialist in these things—named Yolanda Villaseñor. Aunt Lupe wanted to destroy Dodger Stadium. What Yolanda told her was that knocking down buildings could be done, but it was expensive and not too smart. Buildings could be repaired. It was better to place a curse on people. That curse would last.

For six months she consulted with the curandera and worked out the curse. She told me about it and made me promise some things. I didn't think I'd have to do them, but I did.

Aunt Lupe's bulldozed house was right where center field is now. Right on the warning track. She said she wanted to be buried there. She knew O'Malley wouldn't permit it, but for her curse to work she needed to be in the ballpark. She wanted it bad enough that she went against the Church. She left orders to be cremated. Just before she died, she made Freddy Avila promise that he would bury her ashes in center field. Freddy had just started working for the Dodgers as a groundskeeper. Freddy said he would, but after she died he thought it over. He knew about the curse, and he was worried about it because he liked his job. Pretty good pay and he got to drag the infield in front of all those people, twice a game. Freddy decided he didn't want to mess that up, so he refused. And he told all the other groundskeepers and security guards, so we couldn't get near the place. Aunt Lupe thought that might happen,. That was why she made me promise I would take care of it. Those ashes sat in the urn in my kitchen for a long time. I thought about what I could do.

Normal people never get to go on the field at Dodger Stadium, except once. One time. One day a year they let people go on the field.

On July Fourth, 1964, I went to the ballgame. When the game was over, just before they lit the fireworks, they opened the gates by the right-field foul pole and let the crowd onto the field so they could see the fireworks better. I was very patriotic that night. I was the first one onto the field. When enough people had crowded around me and they turned out the lights, I opened the sack that had Aunt Lupe's ashes and I dumped them on the field. Then I, and my thousand co-conspirators, scuffed her into the dirt.

I suppose you want to know about the curse. You might think that she put it on the architects. When Dodger Stadium opened, there were three drinking fountains for 50,000 people. Try to find one even now. And to this day, ask your wife, there still aren't enough ladies' rooms. But that wasn't it. Aunt Lupe wasn't sure that a Mexican curse would work on an Irishman. She did know who it would work on.

She had the curandera put the curse on any Latino who played for the Dodgers. It wasn't to kill them or hurt them, but when they played for any other team, they would play better than they would for the Dodgers. It was a tricky curse, but then baseball is a tricky game; it has more to do with your head sometimes than your arms or legs. A bad bounce can give you an error or it can give you a hit, and all ballplayers are superstitious. When the ball bounces wrong too often, you get down on yourself. It wouldn't stop the Dodgers from having good years, but they wouldn't have great years, because everybody knows you can't win a World Series without good Latino ballplayers playing their best.

The curandera warned Aunt Lupe that a curse that powerful, one that would last for years—for generations—was dangerous.

Lupe said she didn't care, she was going to hell and glad

of it, but the curandera said, It's not just you, what about your kids?

Lupe said, "What are you talking? I would never hurt my kids." She had four daughters—Alma, Berta, Carmen, and Dolores—and they all had kids.

The curandera said she needed to skip at least two generations to protect her kids and her grandkids. The third generation would be safe. The curandera told her she would make the curse now, but it wouldn't have any effect until her first great-grandchild was born. Curses are like earthquakes, she said. The longer you wait, the more powerful they will be.

Lupe agreed to that, and the curandera did what she said she would do. Sometimes, Lupe wondered whether the curandera was stretching things out so the family wouldn't complain about no results. Curanderas have their tricks, particularly when there was a lot of money being spent, and this was a lot. Lupe spent more on that curse than she did on her funeral or her coffin or even her wake, which lasted three days.

I think she got her money's worth, but then I lived long enough to find out.

Lupe's first grandchild, Dulce Gomez, gave birth to Lupe's first great-grandchild, Adelita, in 1988. Adelita looks just like Lupe and has the same fire, muy flamenco. She's smart, but in trouble since first grade.

She was born on October 21, 1988, the day after the Dodgers won the World Series in Oakland. You can decide for yourself whether that curse is working.

I ran into the curandera, Yolanda Villaseñor, last year,

and I had to ask her. I still loved my Aunt Lupe, but I loved my Doyers, too, and I was getting tired of them coming close and then losing. I asked her, Is the curse forever? Can they never win?

Yolanda looked at me like I was questioning the warranty on the new car she sold my aunt. Maybe if they move back to Brooklyn or someplace else, she said. But they can't win in Chavez Ravine.

THE MOON REACHES DOWN FOR ME LIKE THE FIST IN A SIQUEIROS PAINTING

A BOILERMAKER IS an unmixed drink: It's a shot of bourbon or whiskey chased with a beer. Your stomach does the mixing, and something more, I think. Cold fusion or a hallucinogenic reaction, some small rebellion. You sip the bourbon, swallow the beer, and then it kicks back, a slow punt lofted up the neural sheath. You feel it at the base of your skull and think about hang-time as it travels, pleasurably, up to that small patch inside your pate where spine shivers start.

I don't drink boilermakers often. My usual evening drink is bourbon with a splash of water. On hot days I like beer. When I drink beer, I get a comfortable lazy feeling. Bourbon keeps me alert. Bourbon makes me think that I'm thinking.

Boilermakers are a wild man's drink. None of the usual sobriety sensors work with boilermakers. With boilermakers, you are suddenly over that edge, slurring, without a clue that you were close.

I know I'm over that edge when I start eating everything in sight. It's a matter of ballast. Trying for balance. I really don't like to be drunk; I like that nice, loose imaginative stage this side of drunk, and I eat, when I drink, to stay on this side. With boilermakers, though, food doesn't really help. I don't slow down. Even while I'm eating, I keep setting up that shot and a beer.

On the night that I'm thinking of, I'd gone back to Maddy's house. Maddy is my friend Madden. Madden Davis. Maddy wasn't there, but I have a key; he decided, when I started teaching at the university, that I should have a place to hole up. He's a good friend, Maddy. He knows how small a town Loma Linda can be.

I'd just finished office hours—nine hours to talk with fifteen students and look at their new work. Most of them were doing watercolors. There was some catching up to do. I was making up two weeks of canceled office hours.

My mother had been in the hospital. The tumor was malignant. It was confined, they hoped, to the uterine area. She would have radiation therapy, to shrink the tumor and slow the cancer. The doctors wanted to do a hysterectomy after that.

At Maddy's there was beer in the refrigerator, Mickey's Big Mouths. It's a barrel-shaped bottle with a big mouth. After nine hours of talking, I was dry enough to inhale one. The first sip was amazing. Cold, almost sweet, it was a slap at the back of my head and a long, descending shudder. I finished it and opened another.

It was just six. There would be another hour of light. I finished half the second beer and, thirst and dry throat gone, wished it was bourbon. I wanted the clarity of bourbon.

I checked the liquor cabinet. There was a liter bottle of Jack Daniels on the bottom shelf, with about one good shot left. Maddy would have been disappointed. He prefers to anticipate his friends' needs. He takes friendship and hospitality most seriously.

Maddy comes from an old Virginia family, and even though they ran out of money about three generations ago, he still has their generous instincts. He just can't afford all of them all of the time. Maddy's other family inheritances are a wonderful soft accent and more manners than can be used in California.

I considered the whiskey. I wanted a jolt before I drove the freeway. The commute—Loma Linda to my house in Shaky Town—is eighty miles. I've been driving both ways, twice a week, for three years, long enough to know every flicking building, light, sign, and off-ramp, peripherally and by heart. Long enough to be dulled by the drive. The jolt is to change perception, to make myself more interesting, which makes the commute tolerable.

If Maddy had been home, he would have rolled me a joint. I only smoke grass when commuting, to avoid tickets. Maddy decided it would be a good way to slow me down. When I got bored by the commute, I tried to shorten it by speeding up. I'd gotten two tickets, the last a charitable eighty in a fifty-five. One more ticket and my insurance premium would double. Two, and my license would be lifted.

Maddy worked out the equation. Two hits and I drove comfortably at sixty, eyes wide, a buzz in my head, and the wire taut between my shoulder blades. The grass also provided the necessary paranoia. I drove with the constant sense that a highway patrolman was there, drafting along in my blind spot. Waiting for mistakes. Fear kept the wire taut and my foot light.

I poured the shot of whiskey into a short glass, adding a cube of ice. The whiskey tasted sharp after the beer.

I sipped both. When the beer was gone, there were still a few sips of whiskey, so I opened another Mickey's. When the shot was done, there was still two-thirds of a beer. I went back to the closet. In the back, behind the scotch, was a bottle of Old Fitzgerald. Old Fitzgerald sounds like one of those Smart & Final soundalike brands, but it is actually a fine whiskey. I poured a shot of Old Fitzgerald.

I was nearly through the second shot, pleased at the way it was all working out—the whiskey and beer levels now nearly equal and a dead heat in sight—when I found myself in the refrigerator, rummaging through the hydrators.

There was a heel of salami, a half wedge of Swiss cheese, half a pickle. There were Carr's water crackers in the cupboard. I took it all back to the table and started cutting things off and stacking them up.

It all tasted wonderful—that's another effect of boilermakers. After the pickle was gone, I went back and found a hard-boiled egg and some green olives. I cut the egg in half and spooned on a little Russian dressing. I popped olives like they were peanuts. There was still some salami and three crackers when the second boilermaker was gone. I decided, shrewdly I thought, that I should break the beer cycle. I poured a whiskey and water to round everything off.

I believe that I cleared the dishes. I hope that I washed

them. My main ambition, as I recall, was to get on the road while there was still light. It seemed important. It was about seven when I reeled out the door and stared up at the sky.

It was just light. The tops of the palm trees along Roscoe Avenue were distinct, hard-edged against the bright blue sky, but the lower trunks were shadowed. On smoggy days the twilight in Loma Linda is a golden haze. When there is wind, as there was that day, when it is clear, the air is nearly silver colored in the gloaming. I stood by the car with my hands stretched out flat on the roof. There was a light, warm breeze coming down Roscoe, picking up the heat of the pavement and the scent of the orange blossoms. It was exactly seven. The sprinklers in Maddy's front lawn, which are on a timer, dribbled and gasped and spurted, then shot up steady circles of beads. The drops sprang out of shadow, reached their height, glistened there in the remaining band of sunlight, then dropped to the darkening grass.

I watched the light hairs on my arms moving. The air, the beer, the whiskey, the breeze, the twilight—they all had something to do with my contentment. My shoulders felt light. Oiled. The hair on my neck felt the air. Every hair was a sensor, every pore was a nostril.

There was the first taste of the shade in the breeze now. I watched the chill bumps come up on my forearms. Closure. It was easy to get in the car. The seats were warm, and the red leather was fragrant.

I turned on the lights at the first stop sign. My car is an older Porsche, painted light silver—at this time of evening, the exact color of the air, which makes it hard to see. I've learned to turn on the lights.

While I was at the stop sign, I looked ahead. I could see Maddy's Citroen coming toward me on Roscoe. I've never understood why Maddy drives a car as distinctive as a Citroën, with as much trouble as he tries to get into. It's not the kind of car you can park in front of the motel. Not in a town like Loma Linda. Maddy claims it gives him an excuse to visit the city. There isn't a mechanic in San Bernardino County who will open the hood.

The Citroën looked like a sleek blue bubble gliding toward me. Roscoe has potholes, but the Citroën took them without a shiver, the body lifting each time a tire dropped in a hole. The right headlight blinked, though, with every bump, and it struck me that the car was the summary of French engineering: wonderful hydraulics, bad electrics.

Dana, Maddy's graduate assistant, was in the passenger seat. She is as tall and blond as Maddy but has sharper features and bluer eyes. She does not wear glasses, another difference. Dana was looking at Maddy and talking to him. Maddy was looking ahead, smiling to himself or at the descending sun. I've always believed you are responsible for your face by thirty, that whoever you are will show through by that age. I can't understand how someone as complex as Maddy can maintain such a bland and handsome face.

We were both approaching the intersection. I didn't think Maddy would recognize me with the sun in his face. I rolled the stop sign and passed the Citroën while it was easing to a stop.

The lenses of Maddy's gold-framed glasses seemed to flash as I went by. I did hope he hadn't turned to look, but even if he had seen me, I was glad I hadn't stopped. I didn't know how drunk I was or if I was. I knew I didn't want to talk.

At the last liquor store before the freeway, I stopped and bought another Mickey's Big Mouth. I had exact change. I didn't have to say a word. The clerk never said a word, either. He just bagged the bottle, twisted the neck, and handed it over. It was an entirely satisfactory transaction.

Mickey's is not a good beer for drinking and driving. The wide mouth makes it easy to spill. I leaned against the guardrail in the liquor store parking lot and sipped the beer. There was still sun here on the flat.

The empty rattled satisfactorily against the sides of the orange trash can, an underhand lob from ten feet, and I got back in the car. I gripped the steering wheel, hands at nine and three o'clock, and pushed back, settling into the seat.

I shifted down when the on-ramp was in sight. The freeway runs almost directly due west. I turned into the on-ramp in second, then wound through the rest of the gears as I slid across empty lanes. I enjoy the shifting, the crisp sound, the surge after each gear change. I shifted to fifth as I tucked into the center lane, ran it up to eighty, and then backed off. When the speedometer had dropped to sixty, I put my toe back on the gas pedal. The tachometer pegged at 3400 rpm, and the exhaust note became the familiar drone that would carry me to Los Angeles without a speeding ticket.

The glare caught me as I came out from under an overpass and topped the rise. I was driving directly into the sun. I put my sunglasses on. A small and reasonable response. A natural act. It still required thought for me.

These were my first sunglasses. I bought them when I was going to see my mother in the hospital. Californians without sunglasses are probably rarer than native Californians. There I was, a thirty-five-year-old Californian buying my first pair of sunglasses. Fourteen-fifty. I don't know if they are fashionable or if they suit me. They may even be a woman's pair; the lenses are gradated, almost clear at the bottoms, dark blue on top.

The hospital was in the hills above Glendale. The view from my mother's window should have been the Verdugo Mountains, Descanso Gardens, and half the San Fernando Valley. But all you could see that whole week she was in the hospital were thickening layers of yellow-gray smog, banked up around the mountains and buildings like drifting sand. You couldn't see the car lot across the street.

"The watercolor sadness of smog," I tell my students. I do teach art. "You live in a gouache," I tell them. When the smog is really bad in LA, you don't see through it. You see around it or behind it. It's always there like a smudge on a painting or a wash over a watercolor that gives it a melancholy feel. There was that kind of smog all that week, and driving through it, to the hospital, emptied me out. I bought the sunglasses at a drugstore. The display ad on top of the revolving rack said, "Protective lenses." I wore them everywhere that week. Driving, walking, even inside—in buildings. On the freeway, after the necessary attention paid to on-ramps and merging, I could put them on and feel cool, removed, encapsulated. Then turn the tape deck up. Triply safe: inside the car, behind the glasses, surrounded by music.

I suddenly wished I'd brought another beer for the road.

The 215 interchange was in sight. It's one of my markers: ten miles beyond Loma Linda. Five before Fontana. Sixty miles from home.

This is one of the elegant interchanges. The 215 crosses over my freeway, the 10, thirty feet up. Eight lanes on two tracks. Four spiraling on-ramps/off-ramps unite the two freeways. The ramps rise out of the earth. They sweep, tower, curve, bank, recurve, and everything changes as you drive through. It's like tracing a Möbius strip. At sunset, with the orange light behind it, and with the speeding cars and huge trucks changing its shape on the millisecond, the interchange becomes monumental art, more complex and visionary than the earth art documented in museums. I always think they should let the architects sign the pillars. These architects are as unknown as the architects of the pyramids.

This night, in my peculiarly sensitized state, the interchange was beautiful. The backlight, the setting sun, made it overwhelming. Blessedly, there were no other cars. I dropped down a gear and cut my speed to forty, holding the vision as long as I could until I slid under the overpass.

Around Fontana the sun changed. The sun levitated, no longer floating, but up there by will and the force of watchers. The color changed, gold to orange to red and then blood red. A black collar surrounded the orb just before it flattened to an egg and dropped below the mountains.

The doctors couldn't agree about the tumor. The first, a gynecologist, thought it was a young one, fast-growing. The second, a radiologist, thought it was an old tumor. "How old?" I asked, and he'd shrugged. "Years?" I said. "Decades?"

He told me, "I can't speculate, but years certainly."

I asked, "Is this something that would have been spotted on a yearly pelvic and pap smear?"

He looked at my mother, lying back with her hand on the bed rail. She was blinking slowly, her eyes dark and bewildered with pain. Her hand gripped the rail and her head lifted. She was trying to follow our conversation.

The radiologist pushed at his glasses. "Look," he said, "I can't speculate and besides, what's the point?" He forgot his bedside manner. "What's the point?" the radiologist said again. "To make your mother feel bad? She doesn't need that. She needs all her strength to fight back." We looked down at her, this heavy, anxious, sweet-faced woman. Her flesh was slackening, loosening everywhere but her skull. She gazed up at us, seeking an attitude. Her smile was tremulous; her small, perfectly even teeth never quite met. It was as though we were speaking in a foreign language and she could only understand the tension. Above all, she wanted not to be a cause for argument. Her long hair, still naturally dark and still a matter of pride for her at sixty-seven, was caught under her pillow. Her freckles looked gray. Her hair was lank and thinner than I'd ever seen it.

I truly wished I'd bought another beer. I was beginning to feel jagged, the buzz was fading. If I'd had another beer, I wouldn't need to decide whether I really wanted to stop and buy another. It would have been automatic. No thought, no fault, not by choice, sometimes it is important to think so. Sometimes it is important to get rid of the fine-tuning. The sensitivities.

My mother had five sons. She always wanted six, and she always said so. It was one of her litanies. It took her two husbands to have five. The first husband, a bomber pilot, had flown into a cloud over Sicily. He never saw his son. He was a handsome and dashing man, and she never got over his death. Years later she still maintained a separate safe deposit box for his ribbons and Purple Heart and their rings. She wrote to him in her diary. When I was seventeen, I snooped, read it, and was shocked. "My Darling Ernest..." one entry began, the first that I read. It was dated two years after his death. In '46 she married my father. It was not a happy marriage—he was older, European, and demanding—but she had four more sons in seven years. I was the last, and my father died three years after I was born. They were separated at the time.

She went back to teaching at a Catholic grammar school. People tell me she was an excellent teacher and known as a disciplinarian, something she never quite managed with the five of us. Her life centered on her teaching, her sons, and her religion. The other thing she did was let herself go. She put on weight, more than one hundred pounds in five years. It was insulation, I think, layers of safety, a physical sign that she was out of the hunt.

There are times, my mother says, when it would be nice to know a good, considerate man. A gentleman to have dinner with and go to concerts and the theater with. Instead, she has her sons.

I stopped in Claremont to buy another beer. They didn't stock Mickey's at the Circle-K Mini-Mart, so I bought a King Cobra half-quart instead. Next to the cash register was a five-gallon jar, the kind they ship pickled pig's feet in. It was filled to the wide mouth with water, clean water. It must have been distilled or spring water. There were coins on the bottom, a modest swirl. A handwritten sign taped to the bottle said the money would go for suffering children. The clerk, a round, balding Black man, handed me my change. I dropped it in. The dimes made satisfying plips as they went under. "Why the water?" I asked.

"Oh," he said, "people seem to like it that way. Maybe they think they'll get a wish, I don't know."

"Well, somebody needs it," I said. "Someone can use that money."

He smiled. His teeth were edged with gold, fine Us and upside down Us. "Yes," he said, "that's right. You're right."

The dimes have lost their identity, settling on the shifting pile. The water and the coins and the light in the water moved like long crystals as I stared. It was like staring at your reflections in barbershop mirrors. That same skewed feeling.

In the parking lot, I sipped the King Cobra. It's malt liquor, not great but with some bite. The buzz came back very fast, and I understood two things: It wasn't just refraction that shifted perspective in that water bottle, and this wasn't a beer I really needed. I also understood that I would finish it, regardless.

I pulled the antenna up out of the fender and searched for the ballgame.

Fernando was pitching for the Dodgers. With each pitch I imagined his eyes rolling toward first base, until only the whites showed. It was only the second inning.

Surprisingly, his teammates, the hitless wonders, have given him a lead.

The sounds of the ballgame, clear and familiar, are a comfort. Turning on the ballgame is a more natural reaction for me than sunglasses. Traveling music. Better than music. With music, you know what comes next.

It was dark now. The Circle-K sign, a red K on a white, shining plastic cube, glowed like a parachute flare in my mirror as I topped the freeway overpass.

Claremont is five off-ramps long. The next city is Pomona, and then comes the grade, the long hill. On the other side is Los Angeles.

It was clear to me that I needed something to eat. Ballast. If it were not for the ballgame, I would feel like I was hanging on. The gold reflector bumpers thumped beneath my tires when I drifted too far over in my lane. As I started up the grade, the exhaust note flattened out and then almost fluttered. I'd lugged the engine and it kicked back, the way sails will flutter and crack when they are luffed. I shifted up to fourth, the engine snarled and then smoothed as we ascended. The Dodgers have picked up two runs in the bottom of the third.

There are two summits. Between them is a long pass, and on the hillsides overlooking the pass is the newest Forest Lawn Cemetery. As with the Glendale and Hollywood Forest Lawns, there are marble statues and spotlighted replicas of Mt. Vernon and the Pantheon, but here the dead are all buried on slopes. Every grave has a view of the freeway, and the markers look like rows of theater seats. From behind me the rising moon lights the grass.

The real summit. Crossing the crest, the car felt like it squatted and then nosed down. It was warmer on this side. The lights of the San Gabriel Valley twinkled and sparkled, the benefit of dirty air. Strings of red taillights blended in the distance like a time exposure—long, coursing red lines. The flare of brake lights and the stutter of turn-signal lights filtering off to surface streets is like capillary action.

We only found out about the tumor because she needed a ride to the hospital. She had been bleeding two weeks, with some pain. In the third week the pain got much worse and she started to hemorrhage. A neighbor, Mrs. Roybal, persuaded her to call the doctor, then drove her to his office. Dr. Halsey, an old Southern crock, said, "They is a mass in there," and scheduled a hospital room for Monday.

My mother didn't want to tell us. Mrs. Roybal said that my mother had refused to give her any of our phone numbers. She'd found me in the phone book. Mrs. Roybal didn't like going against my mother's wishes, but she thought the family should be involved.

On the LA side of the mountain, the traffic was heavier, and faster. Ten miles an hour more in every lane. There is an In-N-Out Burger at the Francisquito exit. It seemed like the right place to take on ballast. In-N-Out is a drive-through. They make great cheeseburgers—no secret sauce or relish or chili—just very fresh ingredients, and it doesn't go on the grill until you order. Onions if you want them, and I did.

I ordered, and the voice from the speaker repeated the order and then said, "What's the score?" I had to think a moment and then realized he could hear my car radio. "Four to one, Dodgers," I told him. At the pick-up window I turned the volume up so they could hear inside. Valenzuela has been lifted for a relief pitcher, Tom Brennan, known as The Flamingo for his slow and profoundly awkward pitching motion.

The cheeseburger, still steaming when it's handed over, was as good as I remembered. The tomato, unbelievably, was ripe. You could taste it. Nobody was waiting, so I drove around to the speaker again and ordered another cheeseburger to go.

I had told my mother, in the hospital, "This is a hell of a way to lose weight." Her eyes were swimming with pain, but she blinked and then managed a smile for me. The smile was lopsided; one corner of her mouth would not lift. "I suppose so," she said. "It's so strange," she said. "I always feel full." She's lost thirty pounds, but this shows only in her arms and legs and face. Her stomach, beneath the pale green hospital gown, is puffy. Gas, the gynecologist says, a side effect of the radiation treatments. Gas and the tumor. She could be pregnant, that's the shape, the same swell. A boy, of course. It was the gynecologist who made me think of that. He'd held up his cupped hands to show me the size of the tumor. "It's the size of a large grapefruit." His hands, rounding, made a minute adjustment outward. "Or about a three-month pregnancy."

My mother gripped the side-rail of her bed and tried to pull herself up. "What do you want? What do you want?" I asked. She struggled up, her eyes blinking with each small effort. Her mouth was firm, sucked in with resolve. She swung her legs over; her feet would not quite touch the floor. "Just tell me what you want!" I said.

She closed her eyes completely and her face contorted as she cried out, "I *need* to go to the bathroom. I need to hurry!"

I steadied her elbow. She stood and gripped the IV tree. The tree, a stainless steel pole on wheels with the bags hanging from branches on top, moved ahead of her like a bishop's staff. The IV bag swayed, the length of tubing that ends in her arm trailing after. As she shuffled forward, her loosely tied hospital gown split open. I stared at her bruised back, the mottled veins of her legs, and her wrinkled, drooping buttocks. It hit me: My mother is an old woman. The hospital has done this. This, and one other thing. My mother is the most modest of women. The hospital has forced her beyond that. To the real world, perhaps. That's not to their credit.

My second cheeseburger was handed out the window. I put it on the seat and drove across the street to the liquor store on the corner. Jimmy's Liquors, as I remember it. Now Garza's. One more Mickey's.

The town I am in is La Puente. It is a town that I used to know well. My oldest brother, Art, married a girl from La Puente—his first wife, Sherry. I ran with one of her brothers for a while and learned some things. La Puente is an odd town. It's a tough town, but it's not like other barrios in East LA, where the territorial lines are clear and each gang marks and defends its turf. There are no gangs in La Puente. La Puente is an indiscriminately tough town; it's hard on anybody. The town is about a third Paddies (née: Okies) and about half Latino.

I fit in well in my high school days, which is to say, I

looked like everyone else. All the white boys dressed Mexican. We were called Chicano Falsés, or White Beans, and we wore the uniform: khakis with slit cuffs, Sir Guy shirts, and French Shriner shoes, with the toes polished until they looked like glass.

I've never been quite sure how I got from there to where I am now. From painting cars to showing eighteen-year-olds how to draw—when they should be painting cars. It wasn't a straight line, and it wasn't that I was forced inexorably upward by talent. It just happened. I started doing bodywork and paint in high school, on my own cars, then on others to maintain my car habit. I have a steady hand; pinstriping became my specialty. Pinstriping led to cartooning, cartooning led to airbrushing, which, oddly, made me want to improve my line drawing, which led to figure work, which led me unavoidably beyond a high school education. To UCLA, and the joys of watercolor, collage, and oil abstracts. My other adolescent gift, welding, led me to sculpture, then casting. I had just enough talent to lead me up the steps, irrevocably, to air. To where I am, a Freeway Flyer, a half-time teacher at a third-rate school. And lucky to get it. It could have been different. If my mother had not loved education, credentials, and culture. If I'd not had great teachers. If I'd had a little less talent. I could have owned a custom body shop. I could have been locally famous, sought after and well paid for my art and happy craft.

The tumor. I keep coming back and back to that. Carrying it all those years. How could she not have known? What was the seed? When did she sense it? All those years, ignoring her body. Ignoring, particularly, that part of her body.

Maddy, who maintains a Catholic and ironic perspective, put it this way: "Once you close the factory, there's no sense in maintaining the machinery."

There was a lot of action in the liquor store parking lot. Solitary drinkers, squatting in the shadows, two boys in the lighted phone booths, one laughing and jiving, his elbows cranking like mechanical wings. The other had his head and hand flat against the glass as he spoke slowly into the phone with something like desperation. He dropped the receiver and walked away, leaving it dangling. It's always been a town for low-rent drama.

La Puente hasn't changed, but tonight, as I parked, I understood that I no longer fit in. The car in the next parking space was a '72 Chevy, maroon, with wire wheels. It sat about three inches off the ground. The four boys inside wore watch caps or folded bandannas riding low on their foreheads, black sweatshirts or oversize Pendleton shirts. They eyed the Porsche and they eyed me as I squeezed out. For the first time in years, I was aware of my clothes: a green polo shirt, baggy tan L.L. Bean pants with an elasticized waist. And sandals. The sandals are the point of no return. They could never believe I was once a homeboy. They see the clothes, the red hair, the Porsche—it adds up.

Dick Gregory used to say, "Don't you dare sneer at that man's Cadillac. That Cadillac might be 8,000 missed lunches."

I wanted to say the same. I painted this car. I welded the rusted-out sub-frame. I earned it. I didn't pay for it; I earned it.

The driver of the Chevy turned to the boys in the back

seat. "Ese," he said, "check out the hippie."

"No, Vato!" a back-seat boy said, "es un yuppie," and they laughed.

In the liquor store it was the same. I was the only white face there, but the problem was really my clothes. They're not sure what to do about that, beyond hard looks. Everyone did the slow walk while I was in there.

I found the Mickey's Big Mouth. The clerk approved my choice. So I also bought a half pint of Jack Daniels.

Another boilermaker. Well, why not. Back in the car, I lifted the cheeseburger out of the sack and from the back seat of the Chevy, where the window had been rolled down, I heard, "No, Ese. No es un hippie. No es un yuppie. Es un maricon." He used the abbreviated form for stupid people, for fairies.

Without turning, I told them, "Cuidado, señores, cuidado." *Careful, gentlemen, careful.* The heads turn. I lifted the half pint and uncapped it. Nodded. "Muy peligroso, señores, muy peligroso." *Dangerous, very dangerous.*

There was laughter in the back seat, but the laughter had changed. In my favor.

I started the car and backed up. Moving to another part of the lot. The fringe. The dark area between the store, the laundromat, and the defunct self-serve car wash. The right move at the right time, while they were still laughing. Also, I had to piss.

The Flamingo got plucked. It's now a tie game. I turned the radio off.

I stood inside one of the concrete slots of the car wash and watered the wall.

Above the roof of the laundromat, the moon stands up. Huge. Orange. It had cleared the mountains. The moon reaches down for me like the fist in a Siqueiros painting.

My mother is dying. The doctors have set up a course of radiation treatment. To shrink the tumor. After radiation, they recommend a hysterectomy, to cut out the last of the cancer. The doctors held out the hysterectomy as the reward. The hope. My mother is sixty-seven, but that is not the kind of hope you can offer her. She always wanted six sons.

The day the doctors proposed the hysterectomy, on the way home from the hospital, she stopped at the mortuary and made her arrangements. Then the bank. She wanted crisp bills. On her bedside table are three envelopes with money. One hundred dollars for the priest. Fifteen dollars for three altar boys. Another hundred for the luncheon after the funeral mass. In another envelope is a list of the pallbearers she would prefer. Six of her former students. Six boys. Three were her best students. Two were her favorites. Her Rascals. The last name on the list is a boy whose father had been convicted for tax fraud. He was not one of her favorites, but she thought the honor might help him. Most of these six are no longer boys. Two are in their thirties.

The cheeseburger is cold. I tried a swallow of whiskey. It's not the whiskey's fault, but it doesn't taste like it should. When she dies, I won't fit in anyplace.

She sent me a postcard from the hospital:
Thank you for everything you have done for me.
    Love,
    Mother

The postcard put me in a rage and at first, I couldn't think why. What enraged me was that a ride to the hospital, that visits to the hospital, might be enough, that she thought she should be grateful for that.

In my studio there is a portrait I'm working on. It's taken from a photograph: my mother at twenty-six, a war bride, sitting on the lawn with her first baby, my older brother Ernie. She is freckled, lovely, visibly intelligent. She has one hand in her hair, shading her eyes from the sun. The baby is stretched out on her spread skirt. There is a plump mole just above her upper lip, the most sensuous beauty mark I've ever seen.

Such a waste.

One of the boys from the back seat of the Chevy had gotten out and crossed the lot. He pulled his watch cap forward and chucked his chin at me. "Que paso?" he said. "Where'd you learn Spanish?"

I passed over the half pint. "Mi madre. Mi mama."

He looked startled, "She Mexican?"

"No," I said. "No. She was a teacher."

"Oh," he nodded and accepted the bottle.

It is suddenly clear to me that a generation has passed.

He sipped politely and wiped the neck. There is something else he wants, I think. "Yeah. We was surprised," he said. I waited. "We was wondering," he said, "if we gave you the money would you buy us some beer?"

Another moral choice. Yeah, well, you make it up as you go. No matter how old you are.

In the liquor store the clerk was startled. Two twelve-packs of Budweiser and one Mickey's Big Mouth. I hand the beer through the windows of the lowered Chevrolet. We used to call that look dangerously lowered. Many thanks, offers of beer, which I wave off, and the Chevy slinks away. I'm left with the moon.

I pulled out the Mickey's Big Mouth and crumpled the discreet brown bag. *Discreet* is one of those words—like *prestigious*—that still means something in La Puente. The ribbed, barrel-shaped bottle glowed like an emerald with the acquired moonlight. The green liquid foamed in its capsule. I'm done.

I tossed the bottle lightly, up and easy catches in my palm, just pats, then higher, until it smacked, then higher still, until it touched the edge of the moon and I had to use both hands, and then a last toss.

The bottle twirled up like a fat baton and hung in the face of the moon. I let it drop.

My mother used to chide her noisy students this way: she'd clap her hands for attention and say, "Empty vessels make the most noise."

Not always true, Mother.

The bottle smashed on the coarse-grained asphalt, froth and splinters flew. Heads turned in the dark parking lot, someone hung out of a phone booth. They are used to the sound of breaking glass here, but this was a different noise. This was a full bottle. Such a waste.

CON SAFOS RIFA

THERE WERE NINE of them on the roof. They all wore the St. Patrick's school jacket, nubbly green wool with white vinyl sleeves. It was a cold day for March, for Los Angeles, and most of the boys kept their hands jammed in their jacket pockets. The wind reddened the cheeks of the white boys.

From the roof they had a good view of the south gate, the black asphalt basketball courts, the red-dirt running track around the football field, and the fan-shaped sweep of the surrounding chain-link fence—all of the places the boys from Hamilton High School would have to cross on their way to the fight.

They could see the tops of the Hamilton buildings, across the freeway. The Hamilton boys would be ganging in the yard, they would cross through the walkway, the long pedestrian tunnel under the freeway, come down Salsipuedes Street to the edge of the campus, jump the fence there, and cross the football field. St. Patrick's was a new high school, dedicated three years before; this year the school would have its first graduating class. Seven of the boys on the roof were seniors, members of the inaugural class. This was the first fight in the history of the school.

The reasons for the fight were not entirely clear. There had been slurs, casually exchanged since the opening of St. Patrick's, the usual tensions to be expected from proximity, but these had never progressed to a flashpoint before. Few St. Patrick's boys lived in the immediate neighborhood; once school was let out, a half hour before Hamilton was dismissed, most headed for their bus stops. There was only one place that could be considered disputed territory—the huge car and railway underpass below the freeway, adjacent to St. Patrick's. Smokers from St. Patrick's hid there in the morning. Hamilton boys came there in the evening to write on the immense walls of the underpass, but so did many others. Most of the long walls were sprayed with a tripartite running argument between the 42nd Flats, Avenues, and White Fence, three gangs from Shaky Town.

Interspersed, at lower levels, were Hamilton signings. A recent message had been defaced. The original tag said:

Con Safos Rifa, or C.S.R., accompanied nearly every message on the walls. Roughly, it meant: Same on you, anything you write or say bounces back. Con Safos Rifa had been scratched out and a new message appended:

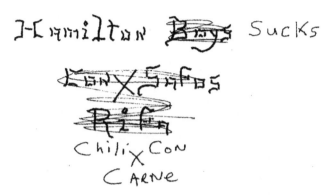

While it was not certain that a St. Patrick's boy had done this, the choice of words and crude lettering style made St. Patrick's suspect and may have been cause for the attack upon two St. Patrick's freshmen: Chuey Limón and Benny Garcia. Chuey and Benny had been beaten up in the tunnel under the freeway that led to Hamilton. There were complications, however. Besides being St. Patrick's freshmen, Chuey and Benny were also lifelong residents of Toonerville, a barrio on the west edge of Glendale, which had a long, historical enmity with the Shaky Town neighborhood, a neighborhood that provided Hamilton with many students. Also, Benny had thrown firecrackers in the tunnel.

The only person who probably knew the actual reasons for the Hamilton–St. Patrick's fight was Frank Sanchez, and Frank was not talking. Or rather, Frank was not clear. The first thing he was not clear about was the actual challenge. He did not say whether St. Patrick's had challenged Hamilton or if Hamilton had issued the invitation. He had simply announced to a number of seniors and a few juniors he could trust that "there's a rumble on. Saturday. Noon. Those punks from Hamilton can't get away with it. We're going to kick their cojones."

Frank leaned forward against the parapet, staring out across the football field. At his feet was an open brown gym bag. Frank prodded the bag with his toe. There was a clink and a dry tumbling rattle as he shifted the bag closer.

The boy next to him, a slight, big-headed boy named Jim Wylie, stared down at the gaping mouth of the bag and the short lengths of pipe and rusty chain. "I didn't bring anything," he said. "I thought it was going to be fists."

Frank was fingering the long hairs in the crease between his mouth and chin. He twirled them together and tugged on them, pulling out his lower lip until it looked like the spout of a pitcher. He nodded solemnly. "What do you think they'll have?" Wylie asked.

Frank released his chin hairs and shrugged. His heavy-lidded eyes and round face were placid. "Same stuff," he said. "Maybe some bats. Some sticks. Aerials. Like that." He prodded the bag again until it clanked. "No knives. No guns. We agreed on that."

Three boys squatted in a corner, backs bent and heads tucked so they were below the level of the parapet, and passed a cigarette. The boy holding the cigarette kept it cupped and waggled his hand vigorously so no smoke appeared, and when exhaling, he blew down into his jacket. The boy who was next to him popped his head up and looked in all directions before hunkering to accept the cigarette. He had a round, flat face, a long neck, and ears that stood straight out from his head, and when he got up to look around again, it made the blond boy holding the cigarette, Kenny Culver, think of something funny.

"Casey," he said, "you look like a fucking radar."

Kenny put his fingers behind his ears, pushing them out like wings, and swiveled his head in small, metronomic jerks: "Radar head."

Casey took a deep drag, squinted at him, and gave the finger.

Behind the smokers, two juniors, John Martinez and his brother, Ralph, sat with the other football players, Don Cherzniak, a heavy, slump-shouldered boy with a spatulate nose—a defensive lineman—and Sandy Furillo. Sandy was a red-haired, handsome boy with the gaze of a collie—a long nose starting high on his forehead and close-set eyes. Sandy was a flanker, the Martinez brothers were offensive linemen. The other three were watching Sandy, who stood in the middle of the roof, swinging a bat. Sandy tapped the bat on an imaginary plate and took his stance, squinting at an imaginary pitcher. His elbow cocked, his front foot picked up, and he strode forward. The bat wheeled in a level, hissing arc. On the next pitch, Sandy squared to bunt. As his hand slid up the barrel of the bat, he changed his mind, and instead of leveling the bat in front of him, he brought it overhead and smashed it down on the graveled roof. Cherzniak's face split in an open-mouthed grin. Frank Sanchez said, "Shut up. Somebody's coming."

Someone was banging up the three flights of steel steps

that led to the roof. Frank leaned over the railing. A short, freckled boy carrying a long piece of pipe had reached the landing just below. Frank said, "Bobby, what are you doing?"

Bobby looked up at him. "Did you see them yet?"

"Where's Reuben?" Frank asked.

"He's still watching the street."

"Get back," Frank told him. "We'll yell if we see them."

They were all at the railing now. They watched Bobby descend and walk back toward the gate. Another boy, tall and frizzle-haired, was there. Bobby waved at him with the pipe: "Get back, Reuben."

"Where are they?" Reuben called. Bobby made a shushing noise, bringing his finger up to his lips. Sandy said, "What time is it?"

The Martinez brothers checked their watches. "Quarter of," Ralph said.

Cherzniak said, "Where the fuck are they?"

Frank said, "We told them twelve. They'll be here at twelve."

Jim Wylie looked around the group, counting. "Do you think anymore of our guys are coming?"

At five to twelve they were all lined along the edge, staring out across the playing field. The wind was snatching up powder from the track, whirling it into dust devils at the north end. Beyond the track was the chain-link fence, the slope, and Salsipuedes Street below. There were two cars parked on the right side of the street; a vacuum cleaner repair van was parked facing them. Otherwise, the street was empty. Twelve exactly. Bobby and Reuben ran up the street toward the south gate, yelling. A green sedan was cruising up the hill, behind them. Two more sedans, white ones, rolled down the center of Salsipuedes Street. All the doors of the vacuum cleaner van burst open, and four men in sweatshirts, jeans, and sneakers ran toward the fence. They scrambled up the slope, hit the fence, and swung over, almost in unison. One man, in a sports coat, remained with the van, standing behind the open driver's door, speaking into a radio microphone. A uniform car came onto Salsipuedes, then another, heading for the tunnel, their lights blinking. "Oh shit," Frank said. He tore open the weapons bag and started dropping pipes and chain down a standpipe. The plainclothes cops were halfway across the football field.

The boys were halfway down as the detective put his foot on the first step and raised the bullhorn. "All right," he said. "You're surrounded. All of you. Come on down." Sandy and the others stopped at the first landing and looked back up. Casey peeked over the side, then the rest of them, led by Frank Sanchez, started down the stairs. They were all down and herded together with Bobby and Reuben, but the detective continued to look up the stairs. He switched the bullhorn on again. "All right. I said all of you. Now!!"

"We're it," Kenny said. "There's nobody else up there." The priest, a pudgy, solemn man of fifty, stood well away from everyone else, on the lawn. He stood with his arms folded precisely, above the swell of his stomach, and watched everything.

The detective jerked his head at two of the cops in sneakers and sweatshirts. "Garber. Swayne." The two unsheathed their revolvers from the snap holsters on the back of their belts and crept up the stairs. As they neared the railing, they flattened close to the wall, and the leader edged up until his eyes were level with the parapet. The roof was flat and without obstruction. His head craned forward until he could see over the parapet and see there was no one hiding behind it. He straightened, stood, and then both of them bounded onto the roof, guns held out. They reappeared, leaning over the railing, "That's all." The detective turned and counted them in disbelief. "Eleven? You're starting a war with eleven of you? Jesus Christ. You're out of your minds!"

"Sorry, Father," he said. This was addressed to the thin, red-haired Brother beside the boys.

The red-haired Brother stared with bright-eyed intensity at the boys. Some were embarrassed and their gazes dropped. "Casey, of course," the Brother said. "Culver, Sanchez, I expected. But Wylie? What are you doing, Wylie? What are you doing, man?" The Brother's face was reddening, and his voice had gone high, tight, and tinny. His brogue was cutting. "And Martinez. Oh, that's very fine. Martinez and Martinez." He turned to the policeman beside him. "The president and vice-president of our junior class." Ralph and John stood silently, two tall, clean-cut boys, their eyes and faces blank. "And the athletes, of course. Oh, that's very fine." He stopped and looked them over, his black pupils wide with anger. "We will talk, gentlemen. We will discuss this in the future." He spun on his soles and stalked away, a tall stick of a man, neck crimson, hands locked together behind his back, his arms a rigid V against his cassock and green sash. The priest watched him go and took out his pipe.

Kenny, who had been looking around, dropped his gaze and nudged the boy beside him, Frank. "Check the roof," Kenny said. "I knew the bastard had to be here." Frank looked at the roof of the main building, where a small man in a cassock studied them through binoculars. "Brother Cyril," Frank said.

The school's dean of discipline had apparently directed the operation; now, as they watched, Cyril beckoned to someone in the street beyond. They began loading the boys into the cars, a random operation. Wylie went by himself, into the front seat of the green sedan, with his hands handcuffed in back of him. Sandy Furillo was handcuffed. Roy and Casey were cuffed, and the three were lowered into the back of a white sedan. The policemen supported them by an arm, guiding them in with a hand flat on their heads, to keep them from hitting the window frame. Bobby was cuffed, Reuben was not, and they went with the unfettered Martinez brothers in the back of the second white sedan. Kenny, Frank, and Cherzniak were led to the last car. The two uniform officers fingered their cuffs and looked them over there. The driver said, "Any of you desperados going to make an escape on us?" He pronounced it "desper-ay-does." Frank shook his head, Cherzniak shook his head, and Kenny said, "No, sir."

The cars backed and turned and rolled down the hill, in a convoy, heading for Eagle Rock Boulevard. On Eagle Rock Boulevard, every place they looked and down every side street, there were boys running—hurdling trash cans, crashing through hedges, hiding behind palm trees. "Look at all those guys," Kenny said. "Did you see that?" Four young men in bulky car coats had burst out of a doorway after the police car had passed them. They broke through traffic and piled into a dangerously lowered copper-colored '51 Chevy.

"Those dudes aren't from Hamilton," Kenny said.

The policeman on the passenger side turned around. "You guys are damn lucky we showed up. You would've gotten massacred."

Frank pulled on his chin hairs, his eyes narrowing into a slow blink. Cherzniak's eyes were wide and startled, his mouth was open, and his tongue moved as he silently counted the running boys and men. A boy in a blue windbreaker skidded around a corner store, arms flailing, the taps on his heels scraping and throwing sparks. He fell, saw them, got up, and sauntered into the store. In the lead car, Jim Wylie put his head down on the seat and cried, "I'm so ashamed. I'm so ashamed."

The detective tried to lift him, "Get up, son. Don't lie down."

"I don't want anyone to see me," Wylie said.

They stopped for the light at York Boulevard, and the detective lifted him by the armpits and set him against the door. Wylie shook his head. His nose was running and tears were dripping from his chin. "I don't want anyone to see me."

The detective said, "You should've thought about that before."

"Oh shit. Oh shit," Wylie said. "My poor mother."

As they neared the Highland Park Police Station, there

was a small traffic jam, a double line of police and plain-clothes cars, each stuffed with boys. There were five and six in some back seats, waving to friends in other cars, giving each other the finger, holding up handcuffed wrists, the hands clasped, shaking them like winners. The double line was squeezing into the station driveway, which was nearly blocked by a large black van. The faces of five or six boys periodically appeared in the grilled window at the back of the van. The van was rocking sideways, swaying on its springs from the impact of bodies, thumping from side to side.

There was a steady procession from the parking lot, policemen shepherding their charges up the steps and through the blocked open double doors. As they climbed out of the car, Cherzniak told Kenny and Frank, "I counted eighty-two and I missed some."

"Most of those guys weren't kids," Kenny said. "Some of those dudes were nineteen or twenty."

They were tramping up the stairs. A uniform officer held them up as they reached the top, "This all of the Catholic contingent?"

"Bring them in here." He ushered them into an anteroom. "I don't want them going in there wearing their colors." The boys looked at him, mystified. "Get your jackets off!" Handcuffs were unlocked, jackets shed. A plainclothesman stuck his head in and looked at them. "Bright boys," he said. There was a scuffling noise, and someone banged against the wall outside. They could hear the plainclothesman talking to someone in the corridor. "Did you see some of those guys? Half of White Fence was out there. So were the Flats, and the Avenues. Uncles, brothers, cousins, granddaddies. You laugh; there was a guy out there with a cane. You take on Shaky Town, you get all three generations. And all we caught were the babies." There was laughter in the corridor. The plainclothesman stuck his head back in and told the uniform officer, "Ready when you are," and then looked directly at the St. Patrick's boys closest to him, Frank and Kenny. "You guys don't know nothing about it, do you?"

The St. Patrick's boys were led back to the corridor and became part of the knot of bodies jostling toward the roll-call room. Inside, a freckled man in a white shirt and a thin tie leaned on a lectern, watching them come through the doorway. He was clean-featured, just starting to bald. The plaque pinned to his shirt said Captain Costello. A uniform officer came in from a doorway at the back of the room. "We're full up in here," he told the captain. The captain straightened, pushing up from the lectern. "Okay. Start filling in the rows here." The St. Patrick's boys were passing through the doorway now. The large room they were entering was walled, with lockers on three sides. Rows of long benches sat behind rows of bench-like tables. The tables had slanted tops, like school desks. Fifty or sixty boys were already seated—talking, laughing, combing their hair, checking out the newcomers. The St. Patrick's boys were dispersed throughout the room. Bobby, Reuben, and Casey were directed to the front row. Sandy Furillo, Cherzniak, Ray Flynn, and Frank sat in the third row. Wylie, pale and distressed, was sent to the back. The Martinez brothers followed him, and Kenny was sent to an empty place in the middle of a row, about halfway back.

Kenny sat down. The boy on his right was dressed in an oversize blue work shirt, stiff and glazed from starch and careful ironing, and pleated, baggy black dress slacks. The shirt was buttoned at the cuffs and neck, and the scalloped tails draped over the pockets of the pants. He was pulling matches from a book and arranging them in a circular pattern, red heads in, on the table. The boy on Kenny's left wore a fuzzy green Sir Guy shirt with a slit pocket and thick, pearlescent green buttons that gleamed discreetly. The nap of the shirt was like mohair and looked as if it had been brushed. It was buttoned to the top, and his thin neck and arms looked frail in the rolled collar and wide half-sleeves. The cuffs of his starched khakis were cut and rolled down. The glassy tips of his French Shriner shoes showed beneath the bell of the khaki bottoms. He was buffing the shoe tips with a folded bandanna. After Kenny sat down, the boy looked up. An imposing pompadour swept up from his small forehead. "Hey," the boy told Kenny. "So howseet going?"

"All right," Kenny said. The boy in back of him was drumming on the tabletop, eyes closed, head jogging. Two rows in front, a boy with a shaved head, wearing an army shirt, was bent low over the table. Within the sheltering crook of his left arm, he was industriously carving, digging into the wood with a small white pushbutton knife. Finished, he swept the chips and splinters to the floor and nudged his seatmate: "Check it out."

The noise level of the room was rising as the police gathered around Captain Costello to confer. Emboldened by this lack of attention, boys stood to yell across the room to friends: "Jesse. Hey, homeboy." "Pinche Pete. Que paso?" "Jesse. Over here, dude." "Nada, man. Still hanging."

Captain Costello broke from the group and returned to the lectern. "Okay," he yelled, "let's settle down." In the comparative quiet that followed, clipboards were passed out to each row. Pencils were attached by strings to the spring clasps and a pad of lined paper was on each board. "You're going to pass these boards down the row," Captain Costello said. "When it reaches you, write down your name, address, and phone number."

"What if you don't got a phone?"

"If you don't have a phone, write down a neighbor's phone."

"Yeah? What if you don't know it?"

"Write down your neighbor's name. We'll look it up."

Another voice called, "Hey. What if you don't like each

other?"

"Hey," the captain responded with irritated mimicry. "That's your problem. We need a phone number. If we cannot locate a parent or responsible relative who will come collect you, then you will sit here."

"Shit. My old man won't come down."

"That's enough."

"I'm going to be here all night. That's bullshit."

"What's your name?"

"Gil."

"What?"

"Gilbert Reyes. Gilberto. Gil. No, use my real name, El Vato Loco." The boy who spoke was the drummer behind Kenny.

"I'll remember you, Gilbert," the captain said. "Now, shut up."

Gilbert grinned at the boys around him. When Captain Costello looked down at the papers on the lectern, Gilbert told them, "He don't scare me."

The captain spoke in a reasonable sing-song, "Shut up, Gilbert. Or you get to sit against the lockers." The captain did not look up. Gilbert grinned again, his eyebrows shifting and his eyes rolling to show his continued courage.

The clipboards crossed the rows. "Print," Captain Costello said. Someone called out, "You want like the last name first and the first name last and that jive?"

"Just write your name, the way you always do. And be sure to print."

When the clipboards returned to the aisle, policemen picked them up and transferred the names, phone numbers, and addresses from the pads to large index cards. These cards were taken to the captain, and he began to call out names, check the information, and ask for more. "Felix Cruz. What's your mother's name, Felix?"

"Linda."

"Your dad?"

"Ernie."

"Age?"

"My age?"

"Your age."

"Fifteen."

"Any nicknames or gang names?"

Felix thought a moment. "El Gato?"

"The Cat? Felix the Cat. Great." The captain wrote it down. "Sandy Furillo. Where's Furillo? How old are you, Sandy? Any gang names or nicknames?"

Sandy thought it over. "The Eagle." Cherzniak reacted with a violent start, jerking his head back to stare at Sandy. "I always liked that name," Sandy told him.

"Don Cherzniak."

"Seventeen."

"Any names?"

"Nah."

"Wait, wait," Sandy said. "Yeah you do. Banana."

"What?" the captain said.

"He eats a lot of bananas. He's known for it."

"Oh yeah," Cherzniak said. "Banana."

Nearly everyone had nicknames after that. Kenny pointed to a large raised patch of keloid tissue on his elbow, the result of a childhood burn. "They call me Scar-Arm,"

Kenny said. Sandy and the other St. Patrick's boys started laughing.

"Scar arm?" Captain Costello said doubtfully.

"Yeah!"

The boy with the pompadour reached out and fingered the scar. "That's really cool. Where'd you get that?"

Kenny looked around them and whispered, "I can't talk about it with cops around."

"Henrique Gomez?"

"Yeah."

"Age?"

"Fourteen."

"Nicknames?"

"Chili Henry."

The boy who'd carved the message on the desk called out, "Tell him your other name."

"Shut up," Chili Henry said.

"It's Maricon."

"Shut up."

"Maricon?" Captain Costello said. "You mean like fairy?"

The carver called out, "The dude's from Mexico, man. First day of school, they ask him who he is and all he says is, 'I American. I American.'"

Chili Henry turned all the way around. "I'm going to cut your huevos off."

The boy to Kenny's right was rearranging his matches in a spiral pattern. The boy with the pompadour nudged Kenny. "That guy, there," he said. Kenny pointed his head toward the boy with the matches and said, "That guy?"

"Yeah," said the boy with the pompadour. "He's been busted three times for arson."

"Arson?" Kenny said.

"Yeah. He rides along on his bike and throws matches into cars that gots their windows rolled down. He burned three of them on his own street. To the ground. To the ground!"

"Pete Madrid," the captain called out. "Where's Pete Madrid?" The boy with the pompadour leaned across Kenny to talk to the boy with the matches: 'Pedro. Hey, they're calling you."

Pedro looked up. "Oh yeah. I forgot. Hey," he said, and raised his hand. "That's me."

"Any nicknames?"

"Uhm. Pedro?"

"Do I know you from someplace?" The captain stared at him.

"I don't know," Pedro said. "Maybe."

"Where?"

"Como?" Pedro said. "Where, what?"

"Where do I know you from, Pedro?"

"Maybe you busted me once. I don't know." Pedro leaned back, latched his hands behind his head, and grinned.

"Pedro Madrid. Pedro Madrid."

The captain repeated the name until it fell into place. He snapped his fingers and pointed. "Bicycle Boy. You like fires, don't you?" Pedro shrugged and continued to grin. The boy with the pompadour was nudging Kenny again. "Hey, you want to see something? Dig this."

The boy raised his left foot and rested the ankle on

his knee. He lifted the slit cuff of his khakis until his sock showed. There was a lump in the sock. He peeled it down to expose the curved pearl handle and chrome hammer of a derringer.

Kenny stared. "Is it loaded?"

"Fucking aye," the boy said. He tugged the sock up and put his foot on the floor.

Kenny nodded, impressed. "You ever shoot it?" he whispered.

"Yeah. It don't shoot too straight. You got to be pretty close to hit something."

"What's your name?" Kenny said.

"Freddy."

There was a commotion behind them. Gilbert Reyes, the drummer, had jumped to his feet and was threatening the boy behind him. The boy had apparently hit Gilbert in the neck with a pencil; he was still retrieving it when Gilbert turned around, Gilbert saw him pulling it back by the string.

"What's going on?" Captain Costello said.

Gilbert jerked a thumb: "This cabrón has got to play. He hit me in the back."

"Reyes," the captain said, "I told you once before to shut up."

"I didn't do nothing," Gilbert said. "It was all this puto."

"No tengo miedo," the other boy said. "Besamé culo."

"That's it, Reyes," the captain said. "Go sit by the wall."

"I didn't do nothing." Gilbert's voice swelled with innocence and injury.

"Move!" Captain Costello pointed to the wall of lockers.

Gilbert shrugged and ambled toward the lockers. "I never do nothing. Trouble just follows me around." He sat down on the floor, his back to the lockers.

"Face the lockers. I don't want to see your face." Gilbert sighed noisily and scooted around. He turned back to give the finger to the boy with the pencil and say, "Fucker. I'll take care of you at home."

"Wylie," the captain called. "Where's James Wylie?" Wylie lifted his pale, pinched face and slowly raised his hand. "Wylie," Captain Costello said, "how come you didn't put down any address or phone number?"

"I don't live at home. I live by myself."

"What's the address?"

"I just moved. I don't know."

"Right," the captain said. "Right. Okay. What's your father's name, Wylie?"

"He's dead."

"What's your mother's name?"

Wylie's head dropped so they could no longer see his face.

"I haven't got time to play with you, Wylie. If I have to, I'll call the school." Wylie shook his head. Captain Costello crooked his finger at one of the plainclothes cops in the doorway. He handed him Wylie's card—"Call the school. Ask for Brother Cyril." The captain read another name: "Anthony Villareal. Where's Anthony?"

Gilbert was twisting a bobby pin in the lock in front of his face. His head rested against the louvers in the locker door, and he was concentrating so hard on the lock that he didn't see the policeman approaching. The policeman snatched him upright by his collar, and Gilbert faced Captain Costello with the bobby pin still in his hand.

"That's it," Costello said. "Cuff him." The policeman pulled Gilbert's wrists together behind his back, clicked the handcuffs shut, and lowered him to face the lockers again. Gilbert arched, twisted his head sideways, and looked down, past his ribs, at the handcuffs and his waggling fingers. He craned the other way to squint open-mouthed at Captain Costello, and after a moment Gilbert addressed him: "Can I talk to my probation officer?"

The names had all been called. The cards were passed to a sergeant and the sergeant went out. Captain Costello went back behind the lectern. He grasped it at the sides and rocked a little, looking at them until they settled down. "Your parents are being called. You'll be released when someone comes to get you." There was a burst of noise, congratulatory and relieved talk and laughter. The captain's face reddened as he shouted at them. "Shut up!" The room quieted. "We will keep your names on file. If you are ever picked up for anything else, this will count against you."

Again the room swelled with noise. Pedro Madrid threw a match at Chili Henry's neck and told him, "See, Baby, I told you they couldn't bust us. What a cherry."

This time the captain waited them out. The noise descended to an anticipatory buzz. His cheeks and the tops of his ears were still flushed. "Nothing happened," Captain Costello said. "So let me tell you what could have happened....

"You could have been shot. You could have been stabbed. You could have had your teeth broken by a pipe.

You could have had an eye whipped out by an aerial. You could have been killed. I've been on gang detail for twelve years. I've seen all those things." The room continued to buzz, and the captain raised his voice. "It didn't happen this time. It could have. Don't trust your luck."

Gilbert, still facing the lockers, made two loud kissing noises. That side of the room began to laugh. The captain slowly closed his eyes and shook his head. Freddy told Kenny, "Oh man. That guy's full a shit."

"Yeah," Kenny said, "cops are always full a shit."

It took a long time for the room to empty. The first set of parents showed in half an hour. There was a gap of ten minutes, and then boys were called out regularly. The boys who remained did not get to view the transfers; the parents were taken to a room near the top of the stairs and the boys were brought to them. Most of the exchanges were quiet. Sometimes there was yelling, weeping; once it sounded like someone rolled down the stairs, and once, the boys were entertained by a female voice screaming abuse at the policemen.

Captain Costello had left the room, returning only to inform Jim Wylie that they had reached his mother, and she preferred that they keep him overnight, so he'd learn his lesson. Bright spots of color appeared on Wylie's cheeks, but his features remained determinedly stony. The four uniformed policemen monitoring the room kept it in good order. Gilbert had been removed. They were allowed to talk, quietly, but as the hours passed and spaces along the benches increased, boredom and anxiety dampened the conversations. Only one parent made it as far as the roll-call room. Frank Sanchez's father, a small man in overalls and a hard hat, his clothes and shoes spotted with tar, pushed through, calling for his son. Frank reached the doorway as his father came in, clutched by two plainclothesmen, who released him there. Frank's father embraced him fiercely and then stared over Frank's shoulder angrily, his eyes sweeping the room and the remaining boys. Kenny was the last St. Patrick's boy to be called out. He waved goodbye to Wylie and followed the sergeant. His older brother, Tom, a recent high school graduate, was waiting at the desk. Tom laughed at the sight of him: "Fucking Kenny."

The plainclothesman who had ragged them on the way in was standing there, leaning against the desk and laughing at something he was hearing on the phone. "Can't believe what they say on these 800 numbers. It's like a two-minute honeymoon," he said. He cupped his hand over the receiver, pointed at Tom, and told the sergeant, "You had better check." The sergeant went to see if Tom was old enough to be considered a responsible relative. The plainclothesman watched them, listened to the phone, and rasped his palm back and forth against the stubble on his cheek. Kenny whispered to Tom, "Where's Mother?" Tom shook his head and looked away from the plainclothesman.

Just behind them, the swing doors leading out broke slightly, joined, and broke again, sucked and released by a draft from the stairway below. The plainclothesman hung up the phone and put his palm on his stomach. "You guys still don't know nothing about it, do you?" The sergeant came back. He had Kenny's school jacket with him. They signed the release, and Kenny was given his jacket.

The sergeant held open a swing door and pointed to the stairs. They stopped on the landing so Kenny could put on his jacket. They heard the plainclothesman talking to the sergeant. "Good Catholic boys," the plainclothesman said. "Good and dumb. They're lucky to be alive."

Kenny whipped around and thrust his fist and upraised finger toward the doors. They clattered down the stairs and went out. It was still light outside. "Where's Mother?" Kenny said.

"She was still at the teachers' meeting when they called," Tom said. "I got the Harrises to drive me down." Mr. and Mrs. Harris were their neighbors, a pleasant couple in their sixties.

"So Mother doesn't know?" Kenny asked.

"Nope."

"Great!" Kenny's heart lifted. He had a quick flash on earlier that day, when his heart had dropped, as the rank of Brothers in their black cassocks and wide green sashes had wheeled around the corner of the school building. It brought him down a little, and then he steadied. It was Saturday. There was still Sunday. The complications and consequences were deferred one day, and for Kenny that was reason enough not to think about them at all.

They went out the gate and once on the sidewalk, off police property, their gait changed to street bop—chins up and pointing, shoulders back, elbows out. Their fingertips were tucked in the front pockets of their jeans. Their hips remained locked. Their knees lifted and broke with each sliding pop and stride. Their shoulders rolled side to side like sailors'. The Harrises' car was on a side street, and they angled that way without once breaking step, making minute adjustments, the necessary slides and skips, without checking. They wheeled around the corner, their knees bobbing together in elaborate cadence. Kenny smiled without looking at his brother, enjoying the feel of the walk, the way they must look to watchers.

A green Mustang on the opposite side of the street wheeled out of a parking place and idled forward. The back window of the Mustang cranked halfway down. There was movement in the shadowed back seat. The snout of a shotgun edged out over the glass. The twin barrels lowered to rest on the glass and probed forward uncertainly, like a mole sniffing the air. The Mustang glided into the wrong lane as it closed on the two white boys on the sidewalk, the shotgun barrels steadied and swiveled, tracking. Then stopped, and kicked up, once and again with the blast of each barrel.

MUERTO MEDINA

IT WAS THE first time that Sergeant Arias had ever gotten sick on the job. He had a strong stomach to begin with and four years on gang detail had made it stronger. It wasn't strong enough for this.

The manager of the Temple movie theater in Highland Park had called in. Arias got there just after the second squad car and before the ambulance. The kid was down on his side in the theater parking lot. They hadn't even gotten him a blanket yet. Arias, kneeling, helped to turn him flat. All three of them gasped. The boy had been stabbed in the face, over and over and over. One eyeball hung out of its socket, dangling over a cheek by the stalk. The other socket was empty, a red crater with jerking nerve endings. His nostrils were slit. The boy's teeth showed through slashed, riddled cheeks and a bubbling bloody froth.

He was still alive, and as they turned him, he whimpered. His mouth opened to a red O and his ruined tongue protruded like a hacked quivering thumb. Sergeant Arias lurched aside, on hands and knees, and threw up his dinner onto the asphalt.

He retched and shuddered until he was only bringing up bile and then, after a diminishing series of dry heaves, he controlled his fluttering stomach. He felt the gentle pat of a palm on his shoulder. "Are you okay, Eddie? Are you okay?"

He nodded his heavy head. He blinked to clear his eyes.

The others had kept their stomachs. He wondered if he'd thrown up for them as well. Then he wondered if it was because he knew the kid and maybe they didn't. The knife had not disturbed the stiff, formal roll of the boy's hair. Sergeant Arias had recognized that pompadour. 42nd Flats. Chuey Medina. He'd been a good-looking boy once.

Miraculously, they'd caught the cutter. When the theater manager had seen what was happening in his parking lot, he'd yelled, and the kid had run. He'd dropped the knife—a six-inch chrome piece of crap from K-Mart—still slick with blood, and trying to pick it up on the run, kicked it. The knife skittered to rest under a construction dumpster at the end of the parking lot, and the kid ran the other way.

With impeccable timing, he'd returned five minutes later, just as the first squad car was arriving. Only his feet stuck out from under the dumpster when officers Howells and Taylor skidded to a stop. The kid was dumb enough to hold on to the knife when they hauled him out by the ankles. According to Officer Taylor, the kid had sat up, clutching the bloody knife to his chest, and said, "I dint do nothing."

When she asked him to hand over the knife, while Officer Howells held a braced gun in view, the kid tossed it forward and said in a voice of outraged innocence, "That ain't mine."

"Not the sharpest machete in the shed," was Officer Taylor's conclusion. "You want to talk to him?"

Officer Howells duck-walked the kid forward and Arias sighed. The new breed—baggy calf-length shorts, oversize Raiders shirt, Converse high-tops, and the badly shaved head. Arias couldn't get used to the burr-head look as a fashion statement. When he was in grammar school, that look had been a mark of shame for second-generation immigrant kids like himself. It signified lice, not style.

The kid leaned forward against Howells's restraint, openmouthed, challenging Arias through half-closed, hard eyes, and Arias sighed. "Way to go, Shorty."

Taylor used her baton like a prod, to move the boy back a little. "You know this payaso?"

"Yeah," Arias said. "He's a 42nd Flats PeeWee. Shorty Chavez. He's Sleepy Chavez's younger brother."

"He's not a PeeWee anymore," Taylor said. "This gets him promoted." She tapped her baton on the boy's shoulder.

"Now you're going to be a full-time Around Town Clown, aintcha, Sonny?"

Howells, nodding his head toward where the paramedics were lifting the limp form of Chuey Medina onto a gurney, said, "Isn't that guy 42nd Flats?"

Shorty Chavez twisted in Howells's grip, spitting with rage. "He ain't Flats!" He strained and stood on tiptoe to yell at the body as it slid into the ambulance. "You ain't Flats, Medina!" He turned to face the cops again as the ambulance door closed. His head twitched and his eyes were unfocused, but he was triumphant and he spoke through a smile. "He's not no Flats. He screamed like a girl. He screamed like a pussy every time I cut him."

EMILIANO PART III: LAST DANCE

THE OLD LADY next door is having a birthday, and she thinks I should come to the party at the Community Center. That's what they call the gymnasium at Coma Park now. It still smells like a gym to me. That old lady is turning seventy-five, and I guess she thinks I should forgive and forget because she's now old and venerable. That was the word her friend the priest, Amadeo, used to describe her when he invited all parishioners to her birthday party, *a venerable member of our congregation.* Socorro said she puffed up like a bird on a cold morning when the priest said that. What I say is that Anita Espinosa has been a cabrona for a lot longer than she has been old, and I would know, she's been my neighbor for almost fifty years. She is three years younger than I am, but she's always been older. When she and her husband, Lorenzo, moved next door, she and my wife, Josie, got to be friends, and I liked Lorenzo. I knew him better than his own wife did, and I still liked him. Lorenzo was a paving contractor, and to get the city jobs he also had to pave the way with the politicians. He knew a lot of bartenders and whores, but he usually made it to Mass on Sunday, and that was enough for Anita. She was religious, and Lorenzo pretended to be, so she thought they were happy until he died.

My wife, Josefina, died long before Lorenzo did. A couple of years after Josie died, I remembered I was a man and I brought some girlfriends home, and that was when Anita started causing me trouble. The old ladies at Cristo Rey started giving me the mal ojo, the stink eye, and even at Las Quince Letras I heard about the chisme she was spreading about me. Then that Filipino priest, Amadeo, came up to me after Mass, right in front of everybody like I had asked for his help. He said he hadn't seen me at church lately. I told him maybe he hadn't been looking hard enough, and then he asked me if I was experiencing doubts about my faith. I said, doubts? He said, yes, doubts about faith and life and was I in need of counsel. I said, no, not at all. I said that every day I thanked the God who had provided me with the fruit of the vine and the joys of women, which made him blush, so I knew for sure where that question had come from.

I talked to Lorenzo about it, and he said he would talk to Anita, but he never did or she didn't listen, so our friendship dried up. The bad news she spread about me kept reaching my ears, so I stopped going to church and planted a eugenia hedge between our houses and let it grow up.

When Lorenzo died and they read the will, it turned out that he left some money to educate a couple of kids that Anita didn't know about. She made some novenas and ignored her own greedy children, who wanted to contest the will, and then she joined the Church full time. It was sad. She was only in her fifties and still a good-looking woman, but she put on the black rebozo and mantilla and started to shrink. You could see the hump grow on her back and her shoulders reaching up for her ears. I still said hello to her when I saw her at Lupe's store or on the street, and I was always polite and friendly right up until the time she was going off to Mass about six in the morning and she saw my friend Socorro leaving my house on her way to work. Socorro is a good woman and a hardworking woman. She tends bar at Las Quince Letras and works the morning shift at IHOP because she's a widow and has three kids, and sometimes out of kindness she also tends to me, and that was her mistake, according to Anita. Socorro nodded and said "Buenos días," and Anita hissed and said, "Sinverguenza!" That was like calling her a whore. I stopped being polite after that. I wouldn't talk to her, and I fertilized and watered the hell out of that eugenia hedge.

The comforts of the Church for old women like Anita will carry them a long way, as long as they are healthy. But sometimes the promise of heaven isn't enough to overcome the pain of this earth. Anita started to feel a lot of pain in her bones and in her joints. I could see that pain when she hobbled down the sidewalk. I know that walk; I walk the same way. When the pain of the arthritis got too bad and the Church's comfort wasn't enough, she remembered what her mother and her grandmother had done and started brewing yerba buena and marijuana tea. I knew that because I saw the marijuana growing up in the middle of her corn. When she started brewing that tea, Anita almost became a real person again. She would smile once in a while and tap her feet to music and not go to Mass every day, and she started to cook again.

That was the one thing she did better than anyone in Shaky Town, even better than Josefina, who was a great cook. Anita had a touch with tamales that couldn't be explained. She did two kinds, pork in a red sauce with citrón and chicken with green chile and Oaxacan cheese and herbs, and both of them would float off the plate and into your mouth, they were so light and flavorful.

She started cooking them for the church, and they would sell out so fast that the priest, Amadeo, raised the price on them from two to an unheard of three dollars. They still sold out and fistfights started in the waiting lines, and then Jacob Silverman, the food guy for the *L.A. Times,* wrote about them. Anita got to be respected for those tamales, and what I said to anyone who would listen was, Good for her. Shaky Town didn't need any extra prayers from old ladies—the ones we already got haven't done much—but those tamales made a difference. Anita made them for the church still, but she did some catering, too, to save up money for her big birthday.

I wasn't going to church anymore, but my niece, Dulcie, would buy tamales for me after Mass. Anita knew somehow. Maybe she looked through my trash out at the curb and saw her knot on the corn husks, or smelled them on my breath when I walked by her house, or someone from Kelsoe's Roundhouse or Las Quince Letras repeated what I said about those tamales, but she knew and she started to tell Dulcie that Don Emiliano didn't have to buy his tamales at the church. If he wanted some, just leave a note in her mailbox and she would leave them on the porch on Sunday, because even if I hadn't talked to her except to say buenos días or buenos tardes in quite a while, I had been a good neighbor and a good friend to her Lorenzo.

Dulcie is like me, she doesn't discuss family business. Dulcie told Anita that she hadn't seen me for a long time, but she would tell me at Thanksgiving or Christmas or whatever the next holiday was, and that was where they left it, until Anita's birthday got closer and she wanted to know if I was coming to the party. She worried about it. She nagged at Dulcie until Dulcie refused to get me more tamales. People stopped me on the street to ask if I was going to the party and why wasn't I going to the party, and all I ever said was maybe and I don't know, and finally I said, Well, I haven't been officially invited, and if she wants me to be there, why doesn't she ask me herself, since I live next door. Then it got back to me that she was afraid, because if she asked me and I turned her down, she thought no one else would come. Old ladies from the church would come, but not anyone looking for fun.

Finally, Victoria Villaseñor, the only one of her friends she knew I would listen to, came by to talk to me about it. I never knew why they stayed friends. Vicky was a pistol. To this day, I don't think Anita understood that Vicky liked ladies. She probably thought that the reason that Vicky ended that arranged marriage at knifepoint was to protect her virtue.

Vicky may have been a virgin, but she wasn't virtuous. Once she held that kitchen knife up to the tender neck of that Valdivar heir, her father's land swap was off, and Vicky, fifteen years old and already knowing what she wanted, fled north to live the life she wanted to live. The Espinosa family took her in, and she and Anita were best friends through high school and beyond, until Anita married Lorenzo. Anita thought Vicky was jealous, but it wasn't that. Vicky knew exactly who Lorenzo was, and worried for her friend.

So Vicky comes by, and she even brings along a bottle. It's Cazadores, which is pretty good stuff, a handsome-looking deer on the label. She pounds on my door and yells, "Emiliano, you going to leave me out here on this porch all night?!"

I wake up and look at the clock. It's not even five in the afternoon. I push down on the footrest of my Barcalounger, and the seat pops up underneath me and I'm propelled to my feet—that's why they're worth the extra money, they lift you like an angel. Meanwhile, Vicky keeps pounding on the door, and yelling, "You going to embarrass me in front of the neighbors?"

I open the door and hold up a hand, "Embarrass you? Impossible."

I haven't seen Vicky in years. She lives in Alhambra, still runs her bar there, and doesn't have any reason to visit. She looks the same, just a little more dried out, like me. Stringy, like carne seca, jerky. Not at all like her friend Anita, who got soft and powdery. Vicky's hair is silver, too, just a little shorter than mine, and swept back the same way. She holds up the Cazadores and says, "I need a favor."

She knows my weaknesses, that Vicky. A favor for a friend who brings a drink with her, who can refuse?

Vicky gives me an abrazo, strong like always, because she knows she doesn't have to worry about me misunderstanding, and she grabs my cheek and pinches it. She tells me, "You look better than you should, Emiliano. Your sins don't show too much."

I wave her to the table in the kitchen and put out the copitas and salt and cut up some limes. She pulls the plug on the Cazadores with her teeth and pours us each a shot and says, "I hope you appreciate me bringing you the best tequila made in Jalisco."

It is añejo, which is rare, and it is reservado, even rarer, but I'm partial to Hornitos. I sip and raise an eyebrow, and she flicks her fingers at me, "It doesn't matter what you think, Baboso. It's already been decided. Cazadores is the best tequila you can buy. Mel Gibson made that movie in Mexico, the one about the Maya. When he was there in the Yucatan, every tequila maker in Mexico sent him a case of their best. When Mel Gibson got arrested in Malibu, guess what he had in the center console?"

"Cazadores?" I ask.

"Cazadores!" She pours us another shot. "So here is what I need," she says. "I need you to go to Anita Espinoza's seventy-fifth birthday party. I don't care what she done. Do this for me. She got fucked up by the church for a while, but she's better now and she's scared to death that no one except the old ladies from the church will show up."

"Is she going to cook?"

"Ayy, Cabrón!" Vicky says. "My first wife, Consuelo, used to say that the way to a man's heart was under his stomach, but I guess that's just young men. Yes, Anita is going to cook. And she is also going to bring in three maria-chi bands. And a full bar."

"She won't need me," I said. "She'll get a crowd."

"She wants the old crowd," Vicky said, from the neigh-borhood. "All the ones who knew her when she was young. She knows they won't come unless you talk to them and let them know you'll be there. It's your duty, as Mayor."

"The old crowd? That means the other three of us left. And who told you about that mayor business? That was when I was drinking more. You been away a long time, you shouldn't come in and insult me right away."

Which is to say, Vicky poured me another shot and lis-tened to my complaints, and I agreed to go to the party.

The night of the birthday party, I have to say, that gym was impressive. Anita did it up right. She had her grand-daughters at the door, who gave you a nice program that made you feel that it was formal, and around the entrance it was packed with flowers and the cards pinned up on the big corkboards. There was a big display of photos of her life. Lorenzo was an impressive man that night. He'd been dead more than twenty years, but you would have thought he'd just been made a saint. There were photos, I swear, of ev-ery sidewalk and curb and street he ever built and ground-breaking ceremonies with smiling politicians. Forty photos of Lorenzo with the golden shovel or cutting through rib-bons, and newspaper clippings, Espinosa this and Espinosa that. I noticed that a lot of those photos were cut, but I was probably the only one there who remembered the originals and knew which girlfriends got trimmed.

Anita was in a few of those photos, but most of the

pictures of her were in front of Cristo Rey Church with her famous tamales or from the long article Jacob Silverman did about how she made them and why they were so good. The photo I liked the best was one where she was looking at Silverman sincerely just after she lied about not using lard in her tamales. Silverman looked like he was ready to cry. I been there on trash day, I know what was out at the curb. Farmer John sells a lot of stuff in gallon containers, but I never saw no label that said extra-virgin olive oil.

Inside was the start of one of the best parties ever. Anita promised a full bar. Vicky was running it, and it was full. They had kegs of Corona in tubs of ice away in the corners of the gym, to keep the kids and cholos away from the neighbors. Vicky had a backlit display of fifty tequilas and anything else you could want. It was like a shrine.

But that's not where you look when you walk through the door. You have to look at Anita and her family. It's like going to church. Against the south wall, across from Vicky's bar, it's like an altar. There are two steps and a platform, all covered with carpet, and on top of the platform is Anita in a big chair, surrounded by her family. As people come through the door, her nieces and nephews are like a funnel, guiding them toward the altar. One of the nieces tried to guide me, but I went to the side to really take a look at things.

You can tell that people are a little surprised. Here in Shaky Town we aren't used to this much organization, but people follow the nieces and nephews, they go to the steps and go up. Some of them look up at the big lights shining down on the altar and look confused. But they are taken to Anita in her chair, and she greets them graciously. Some people have brought presents or flowers or candy. Some poor fools even brought food. Anita's family directs them to the correct table where things pile up, and all I can think is, Anita, who told you to do this?

I head for the bar. And there, awaiting me, holding up a shining shot of Cazadores, if I can believe the bottle next to her, is Vicky. She hands it over. I look at her and I indicate the altar and Anita's family. "Don't look at me," Vicky says. "One of her nieces is a wedding planner."

"Are you being paid for this occasion?"

"Me, personally?" Vicky says. "No. We gave her a discount on the liquor also."

I hand back the Cazadores. "Give me a shot of Hornitos." She winks. I look up at the altar where the people are still being led up. "Doña Anita we can all live with," I say. "But we don't go so much for coronations."

I toss the Hornitos and then follow my nose and all of the people coming down from the altar to the food. The woman can cook. That food is worth everything we have had to put up with in this lifetime and the next. Besides the famous tamales that I've already talked about, there is an excellent green chile corn soup and pechugas con rajas, chicken breasts with green chile in crema. Enchiladas, of course, both red and green. Perfect rice, perfect beans, and at the end of the line, some old friends, Sonia Limón, who has to be eighty-five years old if she is a day, and Mercedes Carriedo, her friend, who is even older, patting out their famous tortillas, Sonia on corn and Mercedes on the more delicate flour. Heavenly morsels. I hug them both.

I take my dinner outside and sit at a picnic table with a

family I don't know, a man and his wife and three kids. We all agree about the tamales being the best, and then the man introduces himself and I recognize him, Luis Romero Junior. His father was a good friend of mine; we even played music together back when I could still play. His wife, Linda, tells me that they were very glad to hear that I had decided to be kind and come to the party. Luis Senior hadn't liked Anita at all because of something she'd said about Teresa, his wife, who was still alive and refused to come. Luis Junior says, "We decided if you could forgive and forget, so would we. So here we are."

By the time I get back to the bar, I'm seeing more and more faces I know. Some I haven't seen in years, and some, like Louie Contreras and Larry Madrid and Del Zamora, that I've never seen anyplace but Kelsoe's Roundhouse or Las Quince Letras.

I ask Vicky for a tray and a couple of copitas of Hornitos and some bottles of Carta Blanca, which is hard to find now. Vicky stocked it special for the viejos. I bring them to Sonia and Mercedes, who are still patting out tortillas in rhythm because people are still lining up for food, some of them, their second plates. "Thirsty work, girls," I say as I set the tray down. Mercedes nods, never missing a beat, she's like one of those lawn birds that clacks in the wind, but Sonia stops and takes a sip of beer. "Thanks for remembering that I like Carta Blanca," Sonia says.

"A lot of memories coming back tonight," I say. There's a tap on my shoulder, and when I turn around I see Anita and Lorenzo's oldest boy, Edward. Lorenzo gave all his kids what he called real American names. Around City Hall he was always Larry, and I guess he thought it would help, if they spent as much time with Anglos as he did.

"Eddie," I say. "Nice to see you." Edward was always a very nice boy, but not well equipped for this world, and it didn't help that Anita pushed him into the seminary when he was only in ninth grade. When he finally got up the courage to quit, in eleventh grade, he never caught up. His friends from grade school had made new friends, and he was shy around girls. I always had a soft spot for him because he and my son Carlos were close before Carlos died. He was gentle, like Carlos, and I know he wanted to be an artist, like me. Tonight, I can tell he is embarrassed. He holds out his hand and shakes mine, but he can hardly look at me.

"Don Emiliano," he says, "my mother would like to thank you for coming to her party. Could I ask you..." and here he gestures toward the stage. I look up. Anita still has a pretty good crowd around her, and more waiting, with presents and flowers.

"Don't worry, Eddie," I say. "I'll be up there. I'm just waiting for the crowd to thin out, so I can have some real time with Anita."

He shakes my hand again and goes up to the stage to convey the message. His sisters close in on him.

Back at the bar, Vicky has to yell at some borrachos pushing in for drinks to clear space. Eddie Goodwin and Marco Martinez have been saving my seat and the bottle of Hornitos that is waiting there. People are having a good time, some of them with full bellies for the first time in a while. Vicky and her helpers are pouring as fast as they can, and it's getting loud and warm. The three mariachi bands are drinking, too, always a good sign. That usually means a long night of good music.

One of the drunks starts yelling for the bands to start. "Give us some music! My ears are cold!" Vicky is on him like a hornet on a piece of melon. "¡Cállate!" She tells him. "We have to hear the speeches first." I finally look at my program and see that Father Amadeo is the master of ceremonies, and only after he gives his speech about Anita's life and good works—and then gives the formal thank-you for her large donation to Cristo Rey and hands over the scroll the Bishop has signed—will we ever get to hear any music. According to the program, though, that was to take place at 7:30. I ask Marco Martinez, the only man among us with a watch, for the time. It is 8:17. Marco is a retired gambler, you might say bookmaker, and he is retired instead of in jail or dead because he was always careful and precise. That means I've been here more than two hours already. The time has gone by so fast.

When I tell that to Eddie Goodwin, he says it's because I'm drinking too slow. Nobody around the bar seems to mind the bad news that we won't have any music. The good news, that we get to drink for free while we're waiting, is enough. Vicky has already had to call her distributor and go back to the bar in Alhambra for more liquor.

I can see that things are thinning out a little on Anita's stage as even the slowpokes have said hello and finished their dinners and started for the bar. I see Mercedes finally starting on her beer and shaking the cramps out of her hands. Sonia has a stack of tortillas in front of her and is starting on her third Carta Blanca.

People are starting to pile up around me at the bar, more old friends, aces I haven't seen in years, and suddenly there is a line in front of me, people waiting to shake my hand and say hello. Tony Mathews is there, the first time I've seen him without sawdust in his hair from his cabinet shop, and Sue Kramer, who taught every kid in Shaky Town how to read. Petrolino Suárez, who owns Tio's Tacos and is probably here because he is still trying to figure out Anita's tamales, jumps in front of a lot of people, like you would expect from a chilango, and shakes my hand. "Emiliano," he says, "Come and see me. We're doing licuados de salud now, just like in Mexico. One with nopales and espinaca, especial for viejos. Come see me!"

One of the Peña girls has fallen over, I can't see whether it is Dora or Gloria. I say girls, but I can say that because they are only in their late fifties. Now I see that it's Dora on the floor and Gloria trying to pick her up, but they are both laughing so hard at something Dora's husband, Jason, said that they can't manage it. The crowd spreads out around them, and I'm looking past them at Anita's stage. All the people are out here now. On stage there is only the family. Anita and her daughters and the granddaughters and young nieces and nephews and poor Edward, the only man among them. All of Anita's brothers are dead, and all the daughters are acrimoniously divorced, so there are no son-in-laws to help out. The niece, who I guess would be the wedding planner, already has a microphone and wants to talk, but they are holding her back. Poor Edward is listening to his sisters and nodding and then looking away. Anita is sitting in her chair and looking up at the lights.

Finally, Edward starts my way, his head down. I stand up and clear the way for him. He has to shout into my ear, "We are waiting for Father Amadeo, but he hasn't come and we don't know where he is. What should I do?" I can imagine the other end of this conversation with his sisters telling him to go talk to the old borracho who is eating up all our food and drinking up all our liquor. "What should I do?" Edward asks again.

I don't even have to think about it. "Eddie," I shout back. "Start the music. Let the mariachis play until Amadeo gets here."

Edward looks at me, helpless. "He was supposed to give a speech."

"Start the music."

Edward shuffles back to the stage, and he tries to get the crowd's attention. He holds up his hands and yells, "Ladies and gentlemen." I think I'm the only one in the place who hears him. I turn around to Vicky and draw a hand across my throat. She stops serving and spreads the word to her bartenders, and then I wave to Linda Sandoval, who is sitting next to her husband, Miguel, who is trying to feed some tamale to their nervous Chihuahua, Fabienne, who is trembling on his lap. Linda has a famous whistle, so loud she can stop traffic. "La Linda," I shout, and put my finger and thumb in my mouth like she does. Linda stands up and stops traffic. It gets really quiet. I point to the stage. "Edward Espinosa has an announcement to make."

Edward steps up, pale and shaking. "Father Amadeo is lost, I guess." That provokes laughs and catcalls. "So until he gets here, we'll have some music." He sits down.

That niece, the wedding planner, is still clutching her microphone, and crying.

I point to the three bands, sitting around drinking, and yell, "Hombres! Do your job. Make us forget who we are!"

It takes a minute or two, but they assemble. I'm pretty sure they've rehearsed or at least talked about it. Each group takes a corner of the room, and when they are agreed and ready, the horn players step up. I know what they are going to do before they do it. Every Mexican does. If there is a "Star-Spangled Banner" for mariachis, it is this song, "La Negra." The first strong trumpet notes purl and halt and build to a measured canter and then break free at a full gallop. It's the Mexican cavalry coming to the rescue for the old and the sad and the sober. If you can hear this song and not move, you have no hips, you have no feet. I can feel myself remembering, with hips that creak and feet that hurt, and I stand up. Young and happy and high again.

Three bands, blending in that high, sweet voice formed in Jalisco, words that make no sense:

> Negrita de mis pesares ojos de papel volando
> Negrita de mis pesares ojos de papel volando
> A todos diles que sí,
> Pero no les digas cuando
> Asi me dijiste a mi,
> Por eso vivo penando

Forty years ago, when Josie and I could afford our first vacation, we went to Ensenada. We sat in Hussong's Cantina, and I paid the mariachis, twelve strong with four horns, to play "La Negra" three times in a row.

They surrounded our table, two guitars, vihuela and

guitarrón nearest, three violins and harp next, four trumpet players backed away, and it was the best stereo in the world. I would have bought more if Josie hadn't confiscated my wallet. Tonight, with three groups, it is almost as good. The room vibrates and people stand and raise their arms and clench their fists and the cries come up. You can see the mariachis remembering who they are. They go through all three verses. No one wants it to end, this old song from Nayarit about the dark woman, the newspaper seller who won't love us. They do the last verse a second time and finally end, with a flourish of trumpets. More gritos come up from the crowd. The horn players have started to sweat, and the gym is now filled with friends and strangers suddenly alive to one another with new eyes and open noses.

The mariachis take turns now, one group trying to top the others, and people start to dance and those at the bar who can't dance or won't dance are still moved.

We won't find out until tomorrow what happened to Father Amadeo, who never shows up. Tomorrow we will learn that Amalia Archuleta, Anita's oldest enemy, both in Shaky Town and at Cristo Rey, where they both have tended the altar for forty years, fighting for crumbs of compliments from priests, had chosen this night to die. Because of her long service to the church, and her insistence, Father Amadeo and only Father Amadeo is to administer the Last Rites. Once he is there at her house, because she won't let go of his hand, and because her large sons and grandsons are attending and insist on respect and comfort for Amalia, we won't know what happened to him until Monday, when we also learn about her miraculous recovery, which Amalia credits to Father Amadeo and his religious powers.

Most of us don't mind Father Amadeo's absence. The music is good, the beer and tequila flow, there are still enough leftovers and salsas and beans and tortillas to put together burritos and tacos if anyone gets hungry. It's only up on the stage that things are tense, where poor Edward is besieged by his sisters, who are driven by their mother's pale and unhappy face.

Poor Edward is pushed from that raft of the stage. He has to swim his way through the sea of the crowd, swaying now to "La Pistola y el Corazón." I watch him struggle to reach me, brought forward on one wave, sucked back by the next. He finally washes in, retrieved by the Peña sisters. They plunk him down on the bar stool next to me. "They want me to make that speech," Eddie says. And he puts his head down on the bar and clasps his hands to his head.

It is at this moment that Vicky Villaseñor arrives and takes away my half-finished shot of Hornitos and my Carta Blanca, and she wipes the bar in front of me with her cloth, looking at me the whole time. She wrings out her bar rag.

"Are you cutting me off?" I ask her.

"No," she says. "I would never do that." She rolls her rag and tosses it over her shoulder. "I just wanted to get your attention." She leans close. "I know this is fun for you. But I would like you to think." She looks sideways to Eddie and switches to Spanish, which she knows he won't understand. "Anita será una cabrona, pero es tu vecina. No seas cruel. No seas imprudente." She is reminding me that Anita is my neighbor and that I have obligations. Vicky puts back my shot glass and refills it and drops down a fresh

Carta Blanca. "Also," she says, "Anita paid for this music and cooked this food that brought you back to life." And then she quotes to me my favorite dicho, one she's heard from me for years: "El diablo no es sabio porque él es el diablo. El diablo es sabio porque es viejo." The Devil isn't wise because he is the Devil. The Devil is wise because he's old.

The Devil would know better. I do the stupid thing. I say, "Come on, Eddie," and lead him to the stage. On the way, I wake up Linda Sandoval and ask her to whistle and she does, unfortunately cutting through and stopping a fine rendition of "Volver." A lot of dancers who were about to reconsecrate some marriage vows there in the dark, split apart. I hated to do it. I love that song. I loved to dance to it. I always loved falling in love for three minutes.

By the time Eddie and I get to the stage, things are quiet. I find the wedding-planner niece and borrow her microphone.

The microphone is a miracle. No wires. I click it on, and everyone can hear me. "Ladies and gentlemen." That's the test and the test works, you can see them turning to listen. "Señoras y señores. Borrachos y borrachas." A laugh and real attention, and I have no idea what to say next. While I am collecting my thoughts, I go to collect Anita, who looks very old at that moment. She looks up at me like she doesn't know what I will do.

I bow to her and take her hand and lift her up from her chair and bring her to the front of the stage. "We are here tonight because of this woman, Anita Espinosa." Everything I have said so far is true, so I go on easily. "I don't know what Father Amadeo was going to say and I don't have any speech prepared." Anita is squeezing my hand, and she looks up at me like I am a doctor or a priest. "So all I can tell you is what I know." I let go of her hand. I have to detach myself from Anita so I can gather strength to tell my lies.

"Anita Espinosa has blessed our community for more than fifty years, as a good wife and a good mother, a good neighbor and a good friend to the church and the poor." People are starting to clap. "And she is a great cook!" Finally back to the truth. The cheers go up, Anita is beaming. Her family behind her is clapping and happy. One more lie.

"On behalf of Shaky Town, Doña Anita, we thank you for being born. ¡Viva Anita!" The cheer is repeated, three times, until Anita is glowing. One more lie.

"To end our ceremonies, I would also like to honor Doña Anita's husband and my good friend, Lorenzo Espinosa. I will ask the bands to play his favorite song, 'Cuatro Caminos,' and ask you all to dance." Absolutely the last lie. I look at the mariachis and say, "Hombres, Cuatro Caminos, suavecito."

They gather themselves in their corners, and at my mark they begin that sad song, the one that always made Lorenzo cry, poor guilty man. I bow to Anita, take her hand again, and lead her to the middle of the dance floor and get her started on that waltz. Two turns in and she's collapsed in my arms, leaning in with her full weight against me and sobbing. She's heavier than I thought she would be. I turn her and turn her once more, so that she is back on her feet, and then guide her to the dark corner of the gym so that her family won't see her crying and blame me.

SHAKY TOWN

I. SPANISH

BROTHER IVAR WHIRLED and threw an eraser. "Burchmore," he screamed, "get out!" Burchmore let go of the T-square he'd hooked over Clark's shoulder and stood up from his tilted drafting table with outraged innocence. His stool fell over behind him. "What'd I do?" Burchmore asked. Brother Ivar, already pink, turned crimson and charged down the aisle, the skirt of his cassock and green sash flailing. Burchmore held his ground until Brother Ivar was upon him and then fled for the door. The class, led by Clark, laughed and jeered as Brother Ivar cuffed at Burchmore, trapped in the doorway. Burchmore clawed at the doorknob until the door opened and he spilled into the hall. Brother Ivar stood over him. "See Brother Cyril after school."

"I didn't do anything," Burchmore said, though they both knew he had. Brother Ivar closed the door and locked it.

Burchmore sat up. The small war with Clark was the culmination of the hazing substitute teachers inspired.

It had started with provocative gum-chewing with loud bubbles, model ball bearings, intended to be measured and drawn but instead rolled to the front of the class, and yelps and belches anytime Ivar turned his back on the class. Burchmore felt justified because, besides being a substitute, Brother Ivar was a lousy drafting teacher, clearly only one chapter ahead of them. The good teacher, Mr. Roach, had left to teach at a public school, dismayed by Catholic-school pay.

Burchmore wouldn't have cared about drafting even if it had been properly taught. It was St. Patrick's concession toward shop classes. The school liked to think that all of its graduates would go on to college, and it couldn't afford trade workshops anyway. Drafting and a photography class were all that were offered for the dim or defiant.

Out in the hall Burchmore thought about what to do next. He was out of cigarettes and the roof wasn't worth risking except to smoke. He had to get out of the hallway. Any priest or brother might catch him loitering and add to his punishment. He peered around the corner. Chris Gonzalez, the school custodian, was standing beside an open classroom door, leaning on his pushbroom. The tools of his trade—buckets, mops, trash cans, rags, and a toolbox—were on a rolling flat-bed cart beside him. Chris was cool, he'd caught Burchmore and Clark smoking on the roof and never busted them, just told them to make sure the stair door was locked when they left.

Burchmore decided it was safest to be next to Chris so he could pretend to help him if anyone official came by. He edged out from the corner and tiptoed up behind

Chris. Chris had his head down, his chin resting on the broom, but he seemed intent. Burchmore understood he was listening, and as he drew closer he could hear what Chris heard. Brother Cyril was teaching his senior Spanish class. Burchmore could see Cyril now, pacing before the class, staring at an open book and reciting. Burchmore hadn't taken Spanish, but he knew Brother Cyril well as the school's Dean of Discipline. In an hour, when the final bell rang, Burchmore would sit in front of him, offer no explanation that Cyril would accept, and be given the usual choice: two hours of detention or five of the best from Cyril's limber bamboo cane. Burchmore always chose the whipping. He valued his time.

Chris lifted his head at Burchmore's approach and held a finger to his lips. "Just listen," he said. The Spanish was not the Spanish that Burchmore was used to from the neighborhood. This Spanish was slower and sonorous, with a rolling cadence and drama, like distant cannon fire. "I could listen to him all day," Chris whispered. "That's the purest Castilian accent you'll ever hear."

Brother Cyril stopped and lifted his heels, going up on the balls of his feet. Perched, he rolled his shoulders, bringing them almost up to his ears, a well-known set of mannerisms that always confirmed for Burchmore the school legend that Cyril had been a famous boxer in Ireland. Trim, snub, intent, he looked like a boxer now as he thrust an open book out to arm's length and held it unwaveringly. "I'll be reading to you now," Cyril said, "from one of Spain's greatest poets, Federico Garcia Lorca. Regrettably murdered by Fascists in 1938, during the Spanish Civil War.

This is Lorca's best-known poem, a lament, 'Llanto por Ignacio Sanchez Mejias.' Sanchez Mejias was a bullfighter, a beloved friend of Lorca's, and the poem was composed just after Sanchez's death in the ring, while Lorca was heart-stricken and grieving.

"Later we will translate the poem, but for now I only want you to listen. The only phrases you might need are 'La Cogida y la Muerte,' which is the title of the first section. 'La Cogida' means 'the wound,' in this case very specifically a horn wound, and 'la Muerte,' is, of course, death. And then there is the repeated refrain, 'A las cinco de la tarde.' 'At five o'clock in the afternoon,' which was the time Sanchez died. I call it a refrain; it is almost a sob when read by Lorca. Simply listen to the sound of the words and you will learn a good deal about the soul of Spain."

"Whoop-de-doo," Burchmore whispered behind the janitor's back. Chris threw an elbow at him. In the classroom Brother Cyril began to stalk the front row until he was ready to read. The corded muscle of his neck, sloping to his shoulders, seemed to flare. "Uno," Brother Cyril intoned, "La Cogida y la Muerte." Burchmore leaned around Chris's shoulder and gave the finger to a boy in the front row he knew, Timothy Coates, but Timothy was entranced.

Brother Cyril's voice rolled and troughed like gathering waves, and even the Castilian lisp was solemn:

"A las cinco de la tarde.
Eran las cinco en punto de la tarde
Un nino trajo la blanco sabana
a las cinco de la tarde
Una espuerta de cal ya prevenida

a las cinco de la tarde

Lo demas era muerte y solo muerte

a las cinco de la tarde."

Burchmore was about to snicker, but he caught the gleam of moisture in Chris's eyes and stayed silent. "That's beautiful," Chris whispered. "You kids have no idea what you're being given here. Poetry puro, man."

Behind them a door slammed open. There was yelling, and then Clark reeled into view, black hair spiked up on one side of his head like it had been yanked. "Fucking Clark," Burchmore whispered. Clark gave him a thumbs-up and then gestured toward the stairway door and pantomimed smoking. "Chris," Burchmore whispered, "we're going to hit the roof."

Chris lifted his chin from his broom and gave Burchmore a look. "Baboso," Chris said. "Tonto. I'm not going to make no excuses for you. You oughta stay here and learn something. Listen to that."

Cyril had reached the end of the first stanza and was in full cry, "Eran las cinco de en todos los relojes! Eran las cinco en sombra de la tarde!"

Cyril stopped, his head bowed. The class was more than quiet, all extraneous noise had been sucked in and held, and they were actively quiet.

"It's like he's a poet himself," Chris whispered.

Burchmore backed away. Clark had the stairway door open and was waiting. When Burchmore was out of reach, he whispered to Chris, "Oh yeah. Oh yeah. I'll try to remember that. When he's beating my ass. At four o'clock in the afternoon."

II. CORPORAL PUNISHMENT

At St. Patrick's High School, in the fall of 1983, the student/faculty handbook listed these duties for the school's Dean of Discipline: *The Dean determines and metes out punishment to students who break school rules. The punishments are temporal—detention, suspension, and expulsion—and corporal—caning.*

When Brother Cyril became the new Dean of Discipline, he believed the job should be as simple as that handbook description, and he had no ambivalence. His own schooling included corporal punishment, and in his career as a boxer he had learned the lasting value of discipline. He had not heard much about the previous Dean, Father Galvin, but he came to know him, in the same way that archaeologists reassemble the lives of the dead.

In Father Galvin's old office, when he unlocked his desk, Cyril learned that Galvin had kept meticulous records of every student who had appeared before him. When he unlocked the office closet, he learned that Galvin favored an array of weaponry.

Staggered in display on a framed pegboard were a whippy, split bamboo cane, a thicker pointer, a sawed broomstick, and an actual paddle. The paddle was a wide, flat thing, like a cricket bat, with holes drilled in its length, for speed was Cyril's guess. At the business end was a decal, a screaming eagle with talons clutched to strike, the symbol of St. Patrick's athletic teams. Vertically lettered on the handle was the motto *Go Eagles!* Cyril lifted the cane down from its pegs, left it on the desk, and locked the rest away.

Corporal punishment, Brother Malachy reminded

Cyril, was always the student's choice. Brother Malachy was the school principal and the man who had appointed Cyril Dean of Discipline. It was late in the fall semester; demerits had accumulated, and the first cases would reach Cyril shortly. Demerits had to be cleared before Christmas. Always ask, Malachy said; if they feared the paddle, they could opt for detention. Very few picked detention when Cyril asked. The trade was three swats for an hour of detention, five swats for two hours. The other brothers encouraged students to pick corporal punishment as the manly choice; detention for a student necessarily meant detention for a brother as well.

The first time Cyril administered punishment, he learned more about the previous regime. The student, a tall and sulky junior named Henry Clausen, was a repeat offender. Henry's widowed mother had indulged him in a car, a cherry red '68 Chevy with white tuck-and-roll upholstery and blatting pipes that thrilled his classmates. The car was supposed to ensure Henry's timely attendance at school—he lived in Boyle Heights, near downtown LA—but what actually happened was that Henry was now tardy two days out of five, because he preferred to cruise Holy Family, a girl's high school in Glendale where the car drew appreciative looks.

Henry told Brother Cyril he couldn't take detention because he had to drive his mother to the store. Cyril doubted that, but what he said was, "Are you ready then?"

Henry looked baffled. "Don't I get to choose?"

Henry was asking about the choice of weapons, and it became clear that Father Galvin had complicated the procedure with odd rules. According to Clausen, if you chose the bulkier paddle, you only received one swat instead of three, or two instead of five. The number of swats went up as the weapon became thinner.

Brother Cyril explained the new regime. "It's two hours detention, Clausen, or five of the best. I use the cane." Cyril used the cane because that was what was used on him. "Which will it be?"

Clausen stood, unbuttoned his corduroys, and let them slip down his legs. He bent over, grabbed his ankles, and waited. Cyril stared at his white cotton-clad backside. "What are you doing, Clausen?"

Clausen looked through his legs. "Huh?" he said.

"Pull up your pants, man. Pull them up."

Clausen levered his pants back up, buttoned, and bent again, and Cyril delivered five whistling strokes.

With each succeeding penitent, Cyril learned more about his predecessor. After lowering his pants and then pulling them back up, Eddie Gonzales told him that Father Galvin had insisted on disclosure even for clothed whippings because a wiseguy once had padded his pants with a towel.

From Tom Koyer, he learned that those who dropped their pants expected lesser blows, Galvin's theory being that the thickness of pants meant he had to swing harder for the same effect. As Tom explained, if you picked the big paddle and dropped your pants, you got a love tap. Pants on, the whack left stripes.

With Felix Rodriguez, Cyril arrived at the final level of excavation. Felix was a departure from the usual penitents.

A small boy, soft and tremulous, Felix was sniffling even before Cyril opened the office door. He held out a rare and immediate pink detention slip, signed by Brother Ivar. "He says I cheated," said Felix, "but I didn't. I just had something in my eye." Cyril opened Galvin's ledger. Felix was a habitual cheater, he'd been caught four times the previous year. There was a note in his predecessor's firm, back-slanted script on the first occasion: *Parental Pressure.* Cyril made a guess. "What's your grade average, Felix?"

Felix wiped his nose and looked at the floor. "C-plus," he whispered.

"And what do your parents expect?"

Felix's head lifted up and his expression was stricken. "You're not going to talk to them, are you? Father Galvin said that as long as I took my punishment, they didn't have to know. Are you going to tell?" His voice trembled and his eyes brimmed. Cyril could scarcely believe the boy was in high school. At the moment he looked about ten years old.

Cyril relented; he wrote his own note below Galvin's— *See about extra-credit projects*—thinking that the boy might improve his grades with extracurricular work. Felix was crying silently now, bent over in his chair and knuckling his face. Cyril touched his shoulder. "We'll keep it between ourselves, Felix. Stand up now."

Felix wiped his face and stood up, hiccuping. Cyril picked up his bamboo cane and Felix turned away. He loosened his trousers and let them drop, then pulled down his checked boxer shorts. He bent over, his eyes clenched shut, and Cyril stared, astonished, at the boy's bared buttocks. "Rodriguez! Stand up. Put your clothes on!" Still bent, Felix twisted around, startled. Cyril prodded him on the shoulder with the cane. "Stand up. Dress yourself."

When Felix was dressed, Cyril sat him down again. "Was that what you did with Father Galvin?" Felix was anxious to please now and talkative, aroused by Cyril's curiosity. "The first time, Father Galvin hit me with the big paddle, and I couldn't stand it. He knocked me down. He asked me if I wanted the cane for the rest of the swats, and I told him I changed my mind and wanted detention. He said he couldn't do that 'cause we'd already started, but then he said he'd hit softer if I wasn't wearing my pants and even softer if I took down my underpants. Father Galvin said the real punishment was the waiting. He had me close my eyes and plug my ears, so I wouldn't know when it was coming. It was awful, the waiting, but then he hardly touched me. Just a tap."

Cyril set the cane down on his desk. Felix watched him carefully, seeking an attitude. "Felix," Cyril said, "I don't want to beat you, but I don't want you cheating ever again. I'm going to ask your teachers to give you extra-credit homework assignments and let's see if we can't raise your grades a bit that way."

"Thank you, Brother Cyril," Felix said. "Do I have to tell my parents?"

"No. No need," Cyril said. He paused, with emphasis. "Unless I learn that you are cheating again. If that happens, they will have to come see me."

Felix's face had lightened until Cyril paused, and then the spark of hope in his eyes turned to ash. Cyril held open the door, "I don't want to see you again, Rodriguez." Felix slipped by him and scuttled down the hall, head down, his hands fisted against his chest. The bell rang, and then echoed on the floors above. Five minutes to two. Cyril locked the office and headed for the stairs and his fifth-period Spanish class.

The only time he had ever met Father Galvin was at the school's end-of-year awards banquet, the previous June. Galvin had returned, from his new parish in Altadena, to give out the awards for Sodality and Confraternity of Christian Doctrine, the two student organizations he had been faculty adviser for. Cyril was there because Brother Malachy had asked him to attend to meet the faculty and students he would be joining the next year, from St. Monica's.

Afterward, Malachy introduced them. Cyril disliked Father Galvin on sight for his enthusiasm. He had an overfirm handshake and a practiced baritone, and he was one of those priests who stood too close to you. Usually they were younger, and Galvin was clearly in his forties and wearing down—his tan was webbed with fine wrinkles and the rose in his cheeks was turning to veins.

Cyril was surprised to learn he was from County Kerry. He'd taken him for a city lout. Galvin was a toucher, not a rural trait. If you were beside him, his arm went round your shoulders; if you were in front of him, he reached for your sleeve or your elbow or touched your shoulder. Some of the boys obviously thrilled to his touch—he had set membership and attendance records with Sodality and Confraternity by intense recruitment and rewards of bowling nights and field trips to amusement parks—and some of the boys just as obviously avoided him.

At the end of the evening, when Brother Malachy walked him to his car, Cyril had asked, "Why is it Kerry men are so daft and have such a high opinion of themselves?" He was only making conversation, but he was curious of Malachy's view of Father Galvin.

"It's beautiful countryside," Malachy said, "Kerry."

"You think that's it, then," Cyril said. "They wake up every morning, congratulating themselves on their genius, choosing to live in such beauty."

"Unlike the clear-eyed sons of County Clare," Malachy said. They were both from County Clare. They'd reached Cyril's station wagon, borrowed from the nuns. "Who wake to beauty and ignore it."

"Differently daft," Cyril said.

Malachy held the door open and Cyril slid in. "Galvin was born in Kerry. But I don't think he lived there long." It was a curiously mild remark for Malachy, Cyril thought, driving away.

After the three o'clock bell, Cyril snagged Malachy on his way out of Algebra. Malachy suggested that Cyril join him on his afternoon constitutional.

They took to the track, the packed red-dirt oval that surrounded the football field. They kept to the outside lane; the track team used the inner lanes for their practice. Whistles, the thud of the shotput, and the clatter of falling hurdles punctuated their conversation.

Halfway through their second lap, Cyril spoke. "Tell me about Father Galvin."

Brother Malachy studied his feet carefully, avoiding the white chalk line marking their lane. "In what way?"

"How did he come to us?"

"He was between parishes."

"Was that usual?"

"No, that was unusual."

"How did it happen?"

"The Bishop asked us a favor."

"The Bishop?"

"Yes, the Bishop." An ungainly sprinter flailed by them on the curve. "The Cardinal was also invoked."

"That's a lot of candlepower for one priest. Why did they do it?"

They were recrossing the starting line for the quarter-mile, and Malachy, a much taller man, was ahead by a stride. He stopped and looked at Cyril. "Father Galvin was undergoing a course of therapy nearby. They wanted to keep him active and useful the rest of the day."

"What sort of therapy?"

"There had been a drinking problem." Cyril, ready to interrupt, sensed a hesitancy and shut up. "And..." Malachy finished, "there had been complaints from parents. He may have served liquor to altar boys. They went on camping trips. Some of the boys said he touched them."

"Oh Jaysus." Cyril was out of diplomacy. "So they send him to a boys' school? And you let them do it?"

"He was held out to us as a man with a drinking problem." Cyril noted how carefully Malachy was speaking. "I didn't learn about the other until later."

They had stopped walking now and stood near the baseball batting cage where the shot-putters practiced. "And how did we learn about the other?"

Malachy linked his fingers through the cross wire of the cage, where a tall, fat boy in green sweats cradled a shot against his bent neck. The chalk on the shot and his hand had powdered his neck white. "Galvin told me. He had progressed enough in his therapy, he said, that he felt the need to tell me. He swore to me that he would not touch one of our boys."

"Except with a cane or a paddle."

"Yes," Malachy said.

Cyril found himself speaking in a furiously measured voice. "Yes. Yes. Felix Rodriguez, this afternoon, bared his ass for me. Yes? A little trick he learned for Galvin. Yes?"

"Felix was never touched."

"You don't know that."

"I do." Malachy pulled on the cage. "I interviewed every boy. Not one of them had been touched."

"Except with the paddle."

"Touched inappropriately."

The shot-putter dipped into a semicrouch, head still cocked to the side, the steel ball pressed between his palm and his neck. "And when you finished your research?"

"I relieved him of his duties as Dean of Discipline. I made a call to the Bishop. They moved him along to his new parish. He's still in therapy. The Bishop says the therapy is working."

"And if the therapy stops working?"

The shot-putter shuffled forward, turning in short, choppy steps. The routine was not ingrained yet, you could almost sense him counting. As his foot nudged the toeboard, he uncoiled and heaved the shot skyward with a grunt and a yell. They looked to see where it would land. The ball thudded down just short of a marker flag, forty feet.

"Good throw, Karl!" Malachy shouted. The boy turned, smiling. "Thank you, Brother," he said, and then looked grave, "but I think I had a foot-foul."

"Looked fine to me," Malachy said.

"Brother Malachy says he didn't see it," Cyril said sharply. "So there's no foul."

Malachy let go of the cage, and ticked off his points on his hands, the way he taught his debaters to do. "One. No boy was touched. Inappropriately. Two. The man has moved on. Three, our standing with the Archdiocese, on whom we depend, has improved. You don't have to think about these things; I do. We've received funds for our chapel, from the Cardinal, two years ahead of schedule. And four. The Bishop comes next May, to consecrate the chapel. The first time the Bishop has consecrated any school chapel in this Archdiocese."

Karl had retrieved his shot and shambled back to the cage. He dropped the steel ball into a flat box of powdered chalk at his feet. A thick puff of the chalk dust wafted toward Malachy and Cyril, and when it reached them, Cyril snapped his head back, as though he'd smelled something acrid. "What's in that chalk, Karl?"

Karl, squatting to roll the ball and coat his hands, looked up mildly. "It's chalk. Gymnast's chalk. It gives you a better grip."

"Thought I caught a whiff of sulfur," Cyril said. Karl looked puzzled. Malachy turned and headed back to the outer lane; he had to skip slightly to regain his stride. Cyril gripped the chain-link of the cage and he leaned in to address Karl. His knuckles were white, and his voice was louder than needed to reach Karl. "Perhaps it's not the chalk. Perhaps it's just out there on the wind."

III. JESUS WAS A CARPENTER

Brother Cyril sat down in one of the deep armchairs facing the fireplace and picked up the copy of *The Tidings* left open on the Common Room side table.

As was nearly always the case, the previous reader had left it open to the announcements page, that section of the archdiocesan newspaper devoted to the comings and goings of the clergy. The newly ordained were listed there, as were the newly departed. Cyril always thought it tactful that the death announcements received the same-size headlines as the appointments, both in the Church's eyes being a form of promotion.

As he scanned toward the bottom of the page, a one-column headline jumped up and bit him:

New Pastor
Named at
St. Anselm's

St. Anselm's had been Father Galvin's parish. There was no mention of Galvin, only the new pastor, a Father McNulty. Cyril scoured the rest of the page and then the rest of the paper. There was no mention of Father Michael Galvin anywhere in *The Tidings*.

The man had unofficially disappeared. No headlines.

No news. Cyril thought of asking Malachy what he had heard but decided to save that.

Cyril looked up the number of St. Anselm's and asked to speak to Father McNulty. When McNulty answered the housekeeper's summons, Cyril inquired after his old friend and classmate, Father Galvin.

There was a long pause and then Father McNulty asked, "Who is this again?" He sounded elderly.

"Brother Cyril at St. Patrick's High School," and McNulty, clearly with pen in hand, asked for the spelling of his name and then asked, "And how is it, again, that you know Galvin?" Cyril duly noted that Father Galvin had become Galvin, which meant he had left the Church. Father McNulty went on to say that he did not know Galvin personally, had never met the man, knew nothing of his circumstances, had himself just arrived, drafted from his parish in Stockton on short notice, following his vows of obedience. McNulty's voice was like a wave breaking on those words, *vows of obedience.* Then he asked for Cyril's phone number and said he would pass the enquiry along to the Bishop, as he was doing with all enquiries regarding Galvin. So there had been others.

Cyril followed the natural lines of enquiry. He called up *The Tidings.* The reporter there, a Mr. Frees, was even less helpful than Father McNulty. The Bishop was again invoked, and then legal precedent. "This is a general policy," Mr. Frees said. He sounded as though he was reading from the boilerplate text on personnel matters: "Because of legal liabilities and to protect the privacy rights of archdiocesan employees, we cannot provide any information as to the status or whereabouts of..."—Mr. Frees paused, and Cyril realized that he would not say *Father Galvin*—"...the man you asked about."

"Then he's left the Church?" Cyril asked. Mr. Frees hung up.

The next policy statement came from Brother Malachy, who asked Cyril to refrain from further enquiries. "I can tell you," Malachy said, "that Michael Galvin has left the priesthood, but that is as much as I know." And then Malachy made an unexpected appeal to Cyril's better nature. He asked that Cyril wait, hold off just a few months on his enquiries—until the final construction work on the new school chapel had been completed and the Bishop had come to consecrate the chapel and say the first Mass there. They were walking on the school's oval track when Malachy made this appeal; the football team was practicing on the green inside the oval. Neither of them paid attention because neither understood the game. Cyril began to understand the weight that Malachy carried, and how much the chapel meant to him. "This is unprecedented," Malachy said. "It is the first time the Cardinal has paid for a high school chapel. It will be the first time that the Bishop has ever come to consecrate a chapel in the Archdiocese. We are being favored. It may very well be because we helped with Father Galvin, but think what it will mean to the school. The Cardinal himself bought the altar and altarpiece, all in Carrara marble."

Cyril snorted, "From the discretionary fund, no doubt."

"Don't disturb them," Malachy pleaded.

Cyril decided he would not trouble Brother Malachy

further; his next round of enquiries would be sub-rosa. He called Captain Costello at the Highland Park police station. Cyril had worked closely with Captain Costello the previous spring to avert what would have been a disastrous gang fight between St. Patrick's and the local public school, Hamilton High. The gang fight had been prevented, but in the aftermath, one St. Patrick's student had been wounded and his brother killed in a drive-by shooting.

Cyril had found Captain Costello to be a true ally in that difficult time, and they had grown even closer in the months since. Captain Costello was a devout but practical Catholic.

They met at the monthly Knights of Columbus meeting at St. Vincent's in Eagle Rock, an excellent cover for them both; it was Captain Costello's home parish and Cyril was an honored guest, come to recruit the K of C sons to St. Patrick's.

In the bar afterward, Cyril explained. "I'm in a pickle," he said. "My predecessor as Dean of Discipline, a Father Galvin, may have sexually abused some students."

Captain Costello stirred his scotch with a finger. "I met the man once. I remember him as enthusiastic."

"I'm trying to track him down," Cyril said. "The man has bunked. I'm getting no cooperation from the Archdiocese. What I hoped was that you could trace him."

"Would you say that there was an active lack of cooperation on the part of the Archdiocese?" Costello asked.

"I would," Cyril said. "It's not that they don't care. Just the opposite."

"Last known address?"

"St. Anselm's in Altadena. The new pastor claims to know nothing."

"Let me make a few calls," Costello said. "I'll get back to you when I know something."

In anger, Cyril had observed, Brother Malachy responded almost like a thermometer: A band of red, first visible at the base of his neck, would ascend until his forehead turned crimson, and a vein throbbed there. When the excitement was more pleasant, Malachy grew pink; his freckles faded, his ears turned rosy, and eventually his face nearly matched his reddish hair.

Today he was pink. The marble altarpiece for the chapel had arrived, seven heavy crates from Carrara in Italy. The two workmen who accompanied the crates, Gerd and Joachim Miller, were local artisans, but their approach and attitude were definitely European. As Malachy excitedly told Cyril, their diamond-edged tools were Swiss and even their cloth tape measures were metric.

The original plans for the chapel called for wood, a good-quality walnut for the altar table, walnut burl veneer for the fascia and cabinetry that would enclose the tabernacle. No saintly relics had been included in the budget. The relic, usually a tooth or the hair or bones of a saint, would be wrapped in lead foil and cemented in place beneath the altar stone during the consecration. Relics of martyrs were preferred but cost extra, and St. Patrick's could not afford that of even a more modest saint.

Then the Cardinal had intervened, providing the five-piece altar slab and four-piece tabernacle enclosure, and also a holy relic, the authenticated hair and finger bone of a St. Basilla, both virgin and martyr. The relics, with their Vatican certificates of authenticity, would remain with the archdiocesan office until the chapel's consecration.

Malachy hovered over the Miller brothers all week, beginning with the hoisting of the crates to the sixth floor—the largest was eight feet by three and weighed four hundred pounds. He oversaw their unpacking, the placement of the carved, beveled marble slabs on the beds of wet concrete troweled onto the wooden forms that the Miller brothers had spent the last month constructing to the measurements furnished by the marble works. Everything fit. All was square and level and in line, plumb as the Miller brothers delighted in showing Malachy. The tabernacle was enclosed. All that remained was the final polish and the placement and cementing of the altar stone above St. Basilla's bone and hair.

Malachy exulted at the craft demonstrated in the marble. "Imagine, man. Just imagine, this was made by workmen whose forefathers quarried blocks for Michaelangelo."

Even with the dust and the lack of polish, Cyril was impressed by the stone and the craftsmanship. The altar table looked nearly seamless, and clearly the five pieces had been cut whole from the same slab, then separated; the delicate green-black veins continued across the joints. The tabernacle housing was the same, with matched veins, and Cyril realized that the cut-out section of the altar table had been sliced into quarters, identical panels, beautifully book-matched.

The only carving was on the face of the altar table, and it was light and delicate, more like engraving than carving, a scrolled filigree with hollowed scallop shells at each corner. It was thoughtful and beautiful craftsmanship, and even if Cyril couldn't truly appreciate its quality, he could sense it watching the solemnity and reverence with which the Miller brothers approached the stone. Both Gerd and Joachim would pause in their labors, stand back and sight along the stone, then run a hand along the surface as though they were stroking the fur of some fabulous beast.

The call came from Captain Costello, and the gravity in his voice alerted Cyril. "Not good news," Costello said. "And you need to understand, before we go any further, that this could hurt you, personally. The Cardinal is cranking up the drawbridge and boiling the oil." He suggested they meet at the Tam O'Shanter on Los Feliz, a restaurant and bar well away from their normal haunts. "I don't think we'll run into anyone," Costello said, "but I don't plan to wear my uniform and I don't think you should either."

Cyril, uncomfortable out of uniform, parked on Los Feliz and walked back to the restaurant. Slacks seemed incredibly confining after a cassock, and he had to resist the impulse to pull down on the crotch.

The Tam O'Shanter, a mock Highlands inn built in the 1920s, looked like a set from *Brigadoon*. A squat round tower topped the low whitewashed building with a conical roof of fake thatch shaped like a witch's hat. The front and sides simulated half-timbered construction, with aged-looking wooden beams protruding from the plaster. A red, many-windowed British telephone booth stood near the portico. Inside, the main room was filled with flags and tartans and heraldry. There were three fireplaces visible with simulated flames and a taped crackle. The waitresses all wore kilts, and the bartender had muttonchop sideburns and garters on his puffy white sleeves. Captain Costello was ensconced in the Snug, a small booth at the end of the bar. He stood up as Cyril was escorted to him by the tartaned hostess. "Mr. Cleary," he said. Cyril had asked for Mr. Costello. As they sat, a waitress immediately brought two drams of scotch, neat, and set them before Cyril. "You'll like that," Costello said. "The famous Macallan, a single malt."

"Did you find Father Galvin?" Cyril asked.

"It's a long and winding tale," Costello said. "We found him. He's in Ireland. No longer a priest. How he got there is a little convoluted." Cyril had his first sip and asked the waitress to bring him water. When she left, Costello continued. "I started with a simple skip trace, Galvin's last address. That was flagged by the boys in Vice and then the DA's office. He was on both of their wish lists. That's where I got most of my information.

"Galvin was in Stockton and Tulare and Anselmo, and he got pushed out at each parish for touchy-feely with the altar boys. They knew they had a problem, but they kept moving him around. Finally they brought him to Los Angeles, to St. Patrick's, while he was also undergoing a course of therapy."

"That was my understanding, corrective counseling, treatment for alcoholism." Cyril sipped again and chased it with water.

"Did it work?" Costello asked.

"May have restrained him a bit," Cyril said. "As far as we know, he did not molest any of the boys in any usual sense. He had some of them undress for corporal punishment."

Costello gave him a long look. "Bare-ass caning? You're right, that's not the usual sense."

Cyril flushed. "I'm sorry," he said. "I'm parroting my principal's phraseology on the matter. This all took place the year before I took the job at St. Patrick's. I was appalled when I found out."

"Brother Malachy," Costello said. "So Brother Malachy calls up the Bishop, they move Galvin out, move him along to St. Anselm's, and things simmer down. For about two years. Then all hell breaks loose. Galvin recrosses the line, only this time, it's the housekeeper's daughter, fourteen years old. Sylvia Molina by name, and she's pregnant. Then he really goes off the rails, tries to talk the kid into an abortion, starts dipping into the collection basket to pay for it. Sylvia freaks, I mean the kid is a devout Catholic. Why else would she be fucking a fifty-year-old priest? She thinks maybe God can forgive her for sins of the flesh, but not for killing a baby. She finally talks to her mother, Inez, and Inez, who is even more devout than her daughter, decides the only thing to be done is to move up the heavenly chain of command. She never even thinks of calling the cops. She calls up the former pastor at St. Anselm's, who is now a monsignor and working downtown. Within the month, Sylvia is living at St. Bridget's, a private facility for wayward girls known for its good soup, kind nuns, round-the-clock medical care, and counseling. Inez continues as housekeeper at St. Anselm's, but she now commutes from her new house in Whittier and her husband, Pedro, has twelve landscaping contracts for churches in the San Gabriel Valley. Galvin, meantime, has disappeared with six months of Sunday collections, which he uses to finance his nervous breakdown. He holes up in a motel in El Monte and starts writing letters to the kids and the parents of the kids he molested in Stockton, Tulare, and Anselmo, confessing in detail as to what he did. They weren't all altar boys. Galvin turns out to be an equal-opportunity predator. There were four girls. He apologizes and suggests that since he can't offer restitution, he would be willing to testify, and admit his guilt, in any civil suit the families wanted to bring. This one is crucial, because the statute of limitations has run out for all these kids in the criminal courts." Costello swallowed his scotch and nodded at Cyril.

"You can guess the rest. These kids aren't kids anymore, most of them are very fucked-up adults, and three of them are dead—one suicide, one drug OD, one from AIDS. The letters arrive, the families go ballistic. Some go right to the local cops, which is how we get the news, but some of them go to their priests, and that sets the really big wheels in motion. What seems to make the Cardinal really crazy is the girls. We've seen this over and over. They look the other way—just a few queer priests, to be expected, doesn't really count—but you get priests who screw anything that moves, that makes them wind up the catapults."

Cyril finished his second scotch and Costello signaled for more rounds. "So the archdiocesan bloodhounds track Galvin down in about two days, we don't know how; took us nearly a week. They seemed to have talked him down off the ledge and renewed his commitment to the Church. All we really know is that they bought him a first-class, one-way ticket to Dublin on Aer Lingus, and an annuity, which continues, and is administrated by the Archdiocese. We don't know any of the details they don't want us to know. The stone wall went up immediately afterward, so all I have is the word of friends in the local constabulary. Galvin now lives happily in Cork. Enjoys the races, I'm told. Has applied for a teaching credential."

Cyril accepted these last words like taps to his forehead, slightly recoiling, his eyes closed, his face now mottled.

When he opened his eyes again, his voice was strained. "Can he be extradited?"

"Not with what we've got," Costello said. "It's only the civil cases now, and Galvin has since recanted on the letters and apologized for his nervous breakdown. There were apparently some settlements for some of the families. We can only guess which, the ones that stopped talking to us. Galvin is a done deal, and you need to forget him. The DA has to concentrate on the cases he has a chance of winning. There are over six hundred."

Cyril blanched. "Six hundred?"

"Did you think it was strictly local? Just the one guy? This was a whole lot of horny priests. Now it's a problem because we can put a dollar number on what it's going to cost the Archdiocese, and if you want to get the Church's attention, all you need to do is present a bill. I found that out in a hurry. As soon as I started asking direct questions about Galvin to the good priests who raised me, I started getting calls from my superiors, asking what the fuck was I doing bothering the Bishop. If they can reach me, imagine what they can do to you."

Cyril suddenly realized that Costello was fairly drunk. Costello's focus and concentration in telling his tale had fooled Cyril.

"I should be ordering dinner," Costello said, "but I'm not going to."

Costello rubbed his nose and then looked hard at Cyril as though he were considering whether to go on. "Two of those cases are from St. Vincent's. My parish. A priest I knew well. The McNally brothers, good friends of my son, Jim. Great kids. I'd never understood why the light went out of them." Costello's broad hand gripped his forehead and his eyes squeezed shut, they opened again, reddened. "I've stopped going to Mass," he said. "Thirty-seven years, never missed a Sunday. This isn't the church I was raised in." Costello stood and fumbled for his wallet, lurched sideways, and caught himself on a chair. The bartender looked up with alarm. Costello steadied himself and winked at Cyril. "I leave it to you."

Cyril watched Costello walk out the front door and then panicked. He couldn't remember how much cash he had on him; he did know that his only credit card was in the slit pocket of his cassock.

The waitress approached, "Would you like another drink?"

"No," Cyril said. "Can you tell me how much we owe?"

"That's all taken care of." She nodded. "The other gentleman."

Cyril drove back to St. Patrick's. He was remembering the scratch and grab of the boys at the seminary, rough and tumble that could turn strange, when you would look into the softening eye of the boy you'd pinned, but that was only friction. You took a shower. Prayed. Jacked off if you had to. Better the venial sin than the mortal. The natural feelings could be acknowledged but not acted upon. Cyril had come late to the seminary, after a flourishing career as an amateur boxer. He hadn't been a virgin, far from it, but he knew many of his classmates were. His commitment had been one of discipline, the same discipline that had served him so well in the ring. It was the way to earn the education he craved, and he had succeeded, earning the bachelor's at Trinity and the two years of graduate school in Madrid. Years later, in Los Angeles, he had been startled to see some of the meek boys of his seminary, confident and entitled, and, he knew, no longer virgins, swelled by their collars.

He knew what would happen if he pursued his questioning on Father Galvin. The questions would double back, his obedience would come in doubt, and he would be looked on as a troublemaker. It wasn't in him to question the Church from the outside, but it wasn't possible from within. And the damage had been done. It might be officially ignored, but the damage had been done. Those kids, to do that to those kids, no matter how fucked up they were, how weak, how willing to please.

The famous passage came back to him, learned in the

seminary. It had been a cautionary tale then, recited repeatedly but never explained: "Whosoever shall offend one of these little ones who believe in me, it is better for him that a millstone were hanged around his neck and he were cast in the sea." No mention of a life-jacket annuity.

All were asleep at the rectory. Brother Cyril tugged off his slacks and sport shirt and drew on his cassock. Flashlight in hand, he unlocked the front door of the school and ascended the stairs to the fifth floor and unlocked the doors of the unconsecrated chapel. He closed the doors behind him and flicked the lights.

He was startled by the brightness. Three powerful new overhead lamps had been installed, one at each side, slanting, and one directly above, highlighting and dramatizing the gleaming expanse of marble. He had been there, the last day, when the Miller brothers had concluded their work, a final cleaning with distilled water and then the final polish with rouges and then a sealant.

What he remembered from that day was that neither Gerd nor Joachim wanted to leave. They found infinitesimal specks on the marble surface to buff out, and then went over the surface a last time with painter's tack rags and a chamois cloth.

Brother Malachy had to finally urge them out the door, reminding them that they would be back to participate in the consecration cementing the altar stone over the remains of St. Basilla. As the Miller brothers backed out the door, Cyril noticed that they were leaving behind their canvas tool bags, slumped in a corner, and pointed this out. They said they would return for them, and it was clear that they wanted reasons to revisit their work.

Gazing now at the altar, Cyril understood their reluctance to leave—it was a thing of beauty, with an austere power.

He unzipped the bags and sorted through them. He drew out a heavy sledgehammer, a broad chisel, and a claw hammer.

All that week in his senior honors English section they had been moving from late-nineteenth- to early-twentieth-century poetry, and Cyril had noted and been slightly bemused by the number of stones and altars and marbles in the poems. He thought the Miller brothers might have enjoyed the class, from Tawny's whited Victorian sepulcher, "that veined stone, beautiful to the eye, which hides the veined corruption within" to Rilke's "Archaic Torso of Apollo," with its famous last line, "You must change your life." Thrilling to senior boys, terrifying to a man of Cyril's age.

Approaching the altar, Cyril lifted the sledgehammer; his right hand slid up the shaft, then slid back to meet his gripping left hand as the hammer wheeled overhead and slammed down on the altarpiece. The stone panel cracked in five pieces, separating in the classic starburst pattern. Cyril broke up the five altar panels with five swings, then used the claw hammer and chisel to pry the pieces loose from the cement that bound them to the screen and plywood beneath. The fragments piled up around his feet as he hammered and pried, cracking in smaller pieces as they hit the pile. His head and hands and cassock were powdered with the white limestone dust. Sweat drew lines through his powdered face and neck as he hammered the lighter panels encasing the tabernacle. They shattered and fell, and he clawed the last clinging fragments into the mound of rubble at his feet. In less than ten minutes, the months of work by the Miller brothers and that of the workers in Carrara was gone.

Panting, Cyril looked at his reflection in the gold tabernacle door. He tempered his fury. Malachy had paid for the door, not the Cardinal. Cyril swung the door open and stowed the Miller brothers' sledgehammer and broad chisel there. He left the chapel, lights blazing, marble dust hanging in the still air, and stalked down the stairway, the claw hammer swinging loosely in his left hand.

He used his master key to open the door to Malachy's office. He sat in Malachy's chair, drew stationery from Malachy's desk drawer, and using Malachy's fountain pen, printed out a message.

Jesus was a carpenter and
wood was good enough for him.

He swept the desk pad to the floor, centered the paper on the desk, and then pegged it there with the claws of the hammer embedded deep in the wooden veneer.

He left it there, left the lights on and the doors open, and walked to the rectory to wash his face and change into civilian clothing.

IV. AT THE DMV

The Hollywood Department of Motor Vehicles was not a happy place. If you were there, you were waiting to explain—a failed smog test, a lost pink slip, trouble with the law. In Cyril's case, it was a problem with his driver's license. Worse, it was self-imposed. He didn't have to be there.

He had spent much time these last weeks in government offices. Employment, Social Security, Immigration, and now, for the second time, the Department of Motor Vehicles. The offices were all the same: a wide expanse of scuffed linoleum with louvered banks of fluorescent lighting above, divided by a long barrier counter. Desks and interviewers were behind the counter. Supplicants sat in folding chairs outside the barrier.

He had been there nearly an hour, and all the sour faces that had greeted him had been called. He was fairly sure he would be next. A tall Black woman stood up from her desk with a paper that might have his name on it. She was laughing, responding to something her deskmate had said.

She came to the counter, looked again at the paper in her hand, and lifted a heavy ribbed microphone to her lips: "Joseph Cleary. *Mister* Joseph Cleary!" It still startled him, hearing his birth name. He still thought of himself as Cyril, the name he'd taken at his ordination. She spoke with practiced assurance and crisp enunciation. Cyril detected elocution lessons and a bit of church in her voice. He rolled his sporting pages and stood up. "Joe Cleary," she said, "are you out there, Joe? Let's go, Joe."

Cyril sidestepped through the narrow row formed by folding chairs to reach the aisle and raised his hand and the rolled newspaper. She lifted the microphone like a trophy and pointed at him with her other hand; her voice was ebullient and welcoming. "Joseph is here. Come on up, Joe!"

A few of the remaining petitioners, scattered in the rows of chairs, gaped at him, and Cyril felt as though he'd been singled out from the audience at a quiz show.

Cyril approached the counter where she waited, and smiled at her tentatively.

She smiled back and waved him though the portal. "Let's go, Joe," she said. Cyril followed her, with some wonder. It was the first time he had encountered any merriment in a government office, any merriment at all. She wore a tailored pants suit, olive, sharply creased, with crisp shoulder pads. Lovely hips.

They reached her desk, which faced another desk occupied by a thinner, younger, lighter Black woman who had scrutinized their approach.

His counselor indicated a chair for him, a light dipping wave of a hand, and introduced herself while he settled. "I'm Mrs. Johnson," she said. "How can we help you?"

"Well, it's complicated," Cyril said.

She smiled at him. "Wouldn't be any fun if it wasn't."

Her deskmate lifted an eyebrow.

"I got my new driver's license some months back, and I need to change the name on the license," Cyril said.

"I thought you told me this was going to be complicated, Joe. Or do you prefer Joseph?"

"Actually, it's Cyril."

The deskmate lifted the other eyebrow.

"I see," Mrs. Johnson said. "Start at the beginning and

tell me the story."

"Well," Cyril said, "I got my new driver's license a month ago, in my birth name, Joseph Cleary."

"And you don't like that name?"

Cyril sat straighter. "It's not that I don't like the name, it's that I don't answer to it. It doesn't sound right. I've had another name for twelve years."

Mrs. Johnson took a harder look, to see who she was dealing with, and Cyril, registering the look, tried to explain. "Up until three months ago, I was a Brother." Mrs. Johnson's eyes widened. Her deskmate snorted and swiveled in her chair. "Wanda got another one."

"I was a member of a religious order," Cyril said. "I was a Patrician Brother for twelve years."

Mrs. Johnson had listened carefully to what Cyril had said, and she reacted in a way that Cyril felt was kindly. She leaned forward toward her deskmate and said, "Manners, Estelle."

Estelle straightened, picked up a pencil, and opened a file, and then Mrs. Johnson reached out her hand and patted Cyril's. "I'm sorry," she said. "Please go on."

It was the first human touch—aside from those he'd paid for and interview handshakes—that Cyril had felt in months. This touch was different, and Cyril, prepared to be irritated by the spread of his business to an audience, was warmed. He became very still, and she finally had to prompt him. "So you left the monastery?"

"We weren't cloistered," Cyril said. "We are a teaching order." He paused again, realizing that he was speaking as though he still belonged.

Mrs. Johnson filled the silence. "Didn't work out, huh? Well, don't worry about it. You can always go back if you want. My minister, Pastor Gordon, quits on us about once a year. Says he gives up on us backsliders! Won't come back until we've pledged enough for new carpets, or a roof, or an organ, or something." Her speech had changed; there were no hints of elocution now, and Cyril understood he was being favored and made comfortable.

"What is it you need? You're okay with the last name? Cleary?" Cyril nodded. "So you just want to go back to your religious name?" Cyril thought of denying his religion, but it was the truth, religious also meant exact and it was his exact name. He nodded again.

She smiled. "So it's Cyril Cleary you want on your license. Am I right?"

"Yes, please."

"I thought you said this was complicated. This is California. You can put any name on there that you want."

Estelle, who had been obviously listening and running a pencil through her hair like a comb, could no longer contain herself. "Any name. We had a God Shamgod in here last week. Not the real God Shamgod, not the basketball player, another guy just liked the name. We had a Bunco Haynes and he changed his name to Bunco Squad. He did."

An eavesdropper two desks over, a tall, bald white man with a turkey neck and a turkey egg for an Adam's apple, turned in his wheelchair. "Remember Frick and Frack?"

"Frick and Frack Taylor," Mrs. Johnson said. "She loved the Ice Capades. When her husband died, she changed her first name. She just wanted to."

Estelle held up two fingers. "We had a Tom N. Jerry and a Heckle N. Jeckle the first week I came to work." She looked to Mrs. Johnson. "What was that one? The woman who works at the World News Stand on Cahuenga, the one with the ten colors of nail polish?"

Mrs. Johnson laughed. "My favorite. Rootie Patootie. She changed it from Molly Bubiuch, which I personally thought was a great California name."

The bald man wheeled over. "And *my* personal favorite, Plenny Wingo, Junior." He nodded to Cyril. "Mrs. Johnson can fix you right up."

"This is Mr. Sheridan, our supervisor," Mrs. Johnson said.

"Phil," the man said, waving a hand at Cyril. "Plenny Wingo, Junior. This was a man who admired Plenny Wingo, who was the world's champion backward walker. Justin Chen was his birth name. The day Plenny Wingo died, Justin came in here."

Estelle stood up. "I remember him! He backed in here with these little dental mirrors taped to his glasses. So he could see behind him. He looked like a guy on a motorcycle backing up on you."

"He hadn't got the hang of it," said Mr. Sheridan. "Said he was going to set all new records, but he was falling down a lot, and whenever he fell down he would stand up and then walk forward until he remembered."

Cyril felt slightly dazzled by their collegial company but wondered whether they would return to his purpose anytime soon. Mrs. Johnson apparently sensed this.

She opened a desk drawer and extracted a triplicate

form with serrations and carbons, which she handed to Cyril. Mr. Sheridan and Estelle withdrew.

"All you need to do," she told him, "is fill out the form with the name on your present driver's license, the driver's license number, and the new name you want on it."

"Just like that."

"You also have to pay the cashier eight dollars. It's no different than if you get married and then divorced and then you want to go back to your married name. Why should we make it hard on you? This is California."

Cyril smiled. "It certainly is."

Mrs. Johnson stood up. "You'll learn. My mother lived most of her life in Louisiana. When my daddy died, she moved here in 1941 and went to work at Lockheed. Emma Thibedoux was as proper and formal as any church woman for her time, but California had its way with her. Before she died, she took tango lessons at Arthur Murray, she saw Duke Ellington in Val Verde Park, she roller-skated at Venice Beach, she took a trapeze class, and she ate avocado soup. She had a date shake in Laguna Beach, she had a margarita in Rosarita, and she wore a two-piece bathing suit."

Estelle, her eyes dancing, was drawing little cheerful circles in the air with her pencil. "Yes, she did. I saw it."

"You better get used to it, Mr. Cleary. You're a Californian, like it or not." Mrs. Johnson shook his hand.

"I know you're right," Cyril said, "but I still have a lot of Irish in me."

"You don't have to give up anything you really want to keep," she told him.

He hated to let go of her hand.

V. FRICTION

Cyril Cleary woke earlier than he would have liked. He'd neglected to trim the blinds, and the sunlight striped him where he lay on the floor. He pulled a sofa cushion down on top of his head to shut out the glare, but the hangover was so bad that the cushion increased the throb.

He crawled to the bathroom, drank water from the bath spigot, and threw up in the tub. He kept the water running and splashed himself, then sank down beside the tub. His head felt swollen and fiercely hot. He pressed his cheek and temple against the tile floor, absorbing the coolness. When he felt steadier, he sipped at the water, and when he kept it down he grasped the edge of the tub and pulled himself up.

He careened to the kitchen, clenching one eye shut and then the other. When he reached the refrigerator, he squinted both eyes against the oncoming light and nudged the door open. Mercifully, there was still a half-full quart bottle of Rainier Ale.

He leaned against the cupboard and tipped the green bottle up with both hands, pushing the tip of his tongue to block the opening. He furled his tongue slightly and a trickle of ale funneled onto his palate. He gagged, held it, then swallowed slowly. The yeasty metallic taste rose into the devious sinal passages of his thrice-broken nose.

His nostrils flared and he had to blink. Cyril shuddered, but the ale descended, past heartburn, to his stomach, which he felt revolving at an infinitely slow rate.

He allowed a second swallow, lowered the bottle, and tried a ginger belch. His eyes clenched as the gas ascended. Tears squeezed out and his forehead glistened, but he didn't throw up.

Hangover wasn't the right word. Hangover was something that happened *to* you. Hangover was passive; what was happening in his head and gut was active and deserved. English wouldn't do, only Spanish would do. He'd earned the *Cruda. Cruda*, the poisonous cherry on top of the day he'd had before.

Cyril had worked now nearly a year for Hoover Vacuums. It was only the third job of his life, following his twelve years as a Patrician Brother and teacher, and before that, his career as a boxer.

He believed thoroughly in the value of the product, and this conviction propelled his sales. He had been promoted the month before. His supervisor, Gus Melling, who was thrilled by Cyril's success, talked about the Blarney Stone and the gift of gab. Because of that success, Melling had the past week moved him into an experimental program. Usually the salesmen worked on leads, but sometimes the company would decide to explore a new territory and knock on every door. Cyril would be paid a dollar and a half for every door he knocked on, whether anyone answered or not. If he was active, he would make more than he could by selling. It was a bonus of sorts.

Cyril decided that he wanted to sell, not just walk the neighborhood, and really knock Melling out. These would be cold calls, which he'd been forced to do as a trainee, and Cyril had done well then, with a method of his own. He would approach the first house of the day and knock, seeking only a name. When the door opened, he would ask for Mrs. Catherine Cleary, who of course didn't live there because she was his mother and lived in County Clare. The householder was usually relieved that this wasn't a sales call, so when Cyril apologized and asked in a friendly way what her name was, "I'm so sorry Mrs....?" she would fill in the blank. Armed with the name, Cyril would knock at the next house. Just as the door cracked open, he would begin his spiel, "Your neighbor, Mrs. Doyle," he would say, "tells me you have a dirty rug."

It wasn't a yes or no question, and that was the genius. Cyril nearly always got in the door. If they admitted the rug was dirty, he was in. If they said there was no rug, he suggested that Mrs. Doyle must have meant the carpet, and agreeing on the old lady's confusion, he was in. If they denied the rug was dirty, Cyril would bring in the vacuum cleaner, with its white paper filters, to clearly demonstrate how filthy the rug was even if it had recently been vacuumed by inferior machines. Filter after filter would be dumped on a paper tray until the virtues of deep cleaning, superior suction, and the best warranty in the business had registered.

When Melling gave Cyril his gift, the only thing that troubled him was the territory. It was near his old school, St. Patrick's, a neighborhood he'd avoided since he'd left. Yesterday he had followed his *Thomas Guide* to the fringe of the territory, Salsipuedes Street.

The name of the street troubled him and not just for what it meant, *Sal Si Puedes—Get Out if You Can*; the name was also familiar. His first stop was the corner house, a pistachio ice cream–colored stucco cottage with peeling white trim and a false tile roof, 402 Salsipuedes Street. The letter box said Slezak. Cyril stepped into the screen porch and knocked confidently. He could smell a burning cigarette. He waited, listening to the whir of a fan, and knocked again. He could see the fan turning on its stalk on the floor next to a couch, and a hand tapping ashes into an ashtray on the bolster; beside the bolster was a tall, sweating can of Schlitz beer. "Mrs. Slezak," Cyril called.

He was startled by the hoarse voice that replied. "Yeah. Who wants to know?"

Cyril declined to give his name. "I'm looking for Katherine Cleary, do you know if she lives next door?"

The Schlitz can lifted and descended, the cigarette glowed in the gloom. "What the fuck?" Mrs. Slezak said. "Who the fuck? That's Madden next door."

Cyril backed out, "Thank you," he said. He picked up his case and backed the gleaming aluminum Hoover upright out from its parking space beside the door and wheeled down the sidewalk and up the front walk to 404, where he rang the bell with merry anticipation. He felt a sale. The door swung back, and even before he could see a face, he was into it. "Mrs. Madden," Cyril sang, "your neighbor, Mrs. Slezak, tells me you have a very dirty rug."

The woman who looked down on him through the screen door, tall and hawk-faced, seemed to swell before him and then she erupted. "That bitch," Mrs. Madden screeched. "She's always telling people I'm dirty." Cyril was nearly knocked down, and while Mrs. Madden rushed to pound on her neighbor's door, Cyril slid down the street, his Hoover wobbling in tow. He skipped 406, because he was still in earshot of the screaming, and then 408, for luck. 410 was around a bend of the street.

410 Salsipuedes Street was a shingled bungalow that looked like it had been added to again and again. The redwood shingles were in different stages of fade. It sat up on the crest of a rise, crowded by knee-high brown grass and fat, stumpy palm trees that leaned against one another. The path that led to the house was cracked cement, overgrown with weeds and baby palms. The porch, supported by tottering brick columns, sagged and a tilted swing hung from one chain. Prosperity and initiative were not the messages given off by the house, but Cyril knocked loudly, through the screen and onto the solid windowless oak of the front door.

There was noise within. As the door swung back, Cyril sang out confidently, "I can smell a dirty rug!" The screen was pushed open, and Cyril was smiling into the face of one of his problem students at St. Patrick's, Raymond Burchmore. Burchmore had clearly been wakened—his pompadour was flattened, and crusted drool caked one corner of his mouth. His puffy eyes widened as he recognized Cyril and then lit with delight. Cyril hoisted his case from where he'd rested it on the porch. He reached behind him for the vacuum cleaner.

When he was the Dean of Discipline at St. Patrick's, Cyril was more accustomed to seeing Burchmore's corduroy-clad backside, bent over and clenched in anticipation of Cyril's thin bamboo cane. Five of the best usually, for tardiness, for disrespect, for fighting, for foul language.

Burchmore was one of those he hated to whip because Burchmore was smart and learned nothing from the lesson. For Burchmore it was a simple transaction, momentary pain rather than what was more valuable: time.

Cyril knew what Burchmore was seeing: the seersucker jacket, the case, and in Cyril's hiding hand, the Hoover, and last, Cyril's shining face. "No way," Burchmore said. His face creased with intelligent humor, and then he started to laugh. It wasn't forced or hollow. Burchmore just laughed. He interrupted himself only once, to choke out, "No one's gonna believe it." He laughed as Cyril turned from the porch and stepped down the cracked concrete path, cutting across the dead grass to the relief of the sidewalk. The laughter followed him at his measured pace for a good distance. Cyril called in sick and said he would need the next day off.

Cruda was the right word, Cyril thought, and so was *borracho*; it was a merrier word than *drunk*, which seemed leaden.

At the Carleton Way liquor store near his apartment in Hollywood, Cyril had revived himself. He liked the place. They stocked Guinness, which was hard to find in this pagan country, and when they didn't, as was the case today, they always had Rainier, the green death. And they didn't mind that he drank in their parking lot. The locals knew him and would leave him to drink in his car while he read the sporting pages. He would pay the tax, a dollar to the first equally hungover supplicant to approach him, and the rest would leave him alone.

He'd had breakfast at Dos Burritos on Hollywood Boulevard, the reliably greasy machaca con huevos. It was strange the way grease helped a true cruda. Now, with a quart of Rainier behind him and a first sip of Jameson in hand, he was ready for contemplation. *The problem with drinking,* Cyril thought, *was that the only time I can think about quitting was when I've had a drink.* He never thought that sober.

Time to move on. There was that other itch, the one that always surprised him, but always accompanied a sincere cruda.

None of the usual girls were out. He'd cruised Sunset twice, Normandie to Western, and none showed. He tried Hollywood Boulevard, which he didn't like because he didn't know the girls there. This close to Christmas, he didn't think the cops would be trying undercover games, but it was best to be careful. He sipped the Jameson in its virtuous Styrofoam cup and turned onto Argyle.

She turned the corner as he turned the corner and gave him a glance. She was very tall, with her dark hair pulled back and drawn into a bun. Her coloring was odd, not quite cocoa, more like a grubby white, but her hair was nappy. The giveaway was her legs, knotty and muscular from long trolling walks, and no mesh of stocking.

Cyril swung around the block and came round again. She had lingered at the Yucca intersection and followed him to the curb when he pulled over. The company car, a Mercury Montego that he found personally embarrassing, was reassuring to most of the girls.

She opened the door and deposited herself gracefully, then slumped in the seat and looked at him. Even slumped, she was very tall. "You ain't a cop are you?" she asked.

Cyril gently accelerated away from the curb. "Fear not," he said, "and I'll do anything you need to reassure you." Her nail polish, which was purple, seemed artfully chipped and disturbing, but then he remembered he was drunk and brilliantly overfocusing. He offered her the Jameson. She smelled it and left it in his hand.

Her name was Lucille and her apartment, which she preferred to you wasting your money on them cheap motels, was in Koreatown.

Cyril turned right on Western and drifted into an area where the signage appeared vaguely English, but on second glance seemed humped and deranged, a language made of Ms and Ys and Us up and upside down.

There was a parking space directly in front of her building. Cyril installed four optimistic quarters in the meter, enough for two hours, and followed her in, focused but not quite able to absorb the machinations of her ass. Doors opened along the corridor as they walked to her room and then closed in disappointment behind them.

Her room was dim and close, dominated by the bed on which Cyril sprawled. "I hate to negotiate," Cyril said, "but I like to come twice." He handed her the forty dollars; one of the things he'd learned early was that all street transactions were now determined by ATM currency, multiples of twenty.

He liked that she was modest. She chose to undress in

the corner, turned a bit sideways. Her breasts were small but beautiful and pointed. As she took off her panties, she turned her back. She paused with her back toward him and gave a small shaking movement, almost a ripple. It might be her ritual, Cyril thought, her preparing. She brought her arms back behind her. Her hands were balled and then she flicked them open, like a dancer. She turned and walked oddly toward him, with tiny mincing steps, almost a shuffle. She swayed when she reached the bed and dropped onto it with a sizable thump.

Cyril reached for her. His head bent to her small dark nipples and his hand slid to her groin. He licked her right breast and his hand moved down over her pubic mound and began the descent between her legs.

"Jesus Christ!" Cyril said. He sat upright. "You should have said!"

"Thought you knew, baby," she said. "Thought I was what you had in mind."

Thank God she'd not been hard, Cyril was thinking. I don't know if I could have dealt with that. And the other side of that coin was: that means she didn't fancy him. Which was worse?

"Why don't I just suck you off," she said.

Her cock was clearly visible now, the pause and the turn had been to tuck it behind her, and that explained the odd, almost geisha-like shuffle toward him.

Cyril took a swallow of Jameson and knelt before her supine body on the bed, his eyes closed. She took him in hand and took him in. It felt good, but when he'd swollen, he became aware of the noises. He knew that noise, he'd spent much time around the elderly and recognized the odd grinding sound of false teeth, slipping in place. He could remember his mother making that noise, idly as she rocked and knitted. Cyril's eyes opened and he looked down. She really was large.

"Could you take your teeth out?" Cyril said.

She looked up at him and let him drop. "I promised my boyfren' I'd only do that for him."

"Ah," Cyril said. "Where are we then?"

She rolled over on her stomach and stirred suggestively. "Why don't you just fuck me."

"What's it like?"

"Well *I* wouldn't know, but peoples tell me it's like a pussy, only tighter."

She reached behind her and spread her cheeks. Cyril stared down at the furrowed brown corona. It was wider and more relaxed than he would have expected. She burrowed into the pillow beneath her chin. "It's all just friction, honey."

Cyril thought of the excited sailor's explanation in *Fanny Hill,* for entering the wrong orifice, "Any port in a storm, ma'am."

He tried, but he wasn't hard enough to penetrate.

"Don't we need some lubricant?" Cyril asked.

"Just spit. Spit's enough."

Cyril spat, but the moisture didn't help. He gave up and lowered himself to slide back and forth between her cheeks. After a time he understood it was useless and stopped.

She turned her head, "You done?"

Cyril slid off of her and reached for his Jameson.

She stirred with new energy, got up, and put on a wrapper.

She retrieved the two bills Cyril had given her and tucked them in her wrapper pocket.

"Is there a way I could have known?" Cyril asked.

She stood, profiled, and smiled, then lifted her chin and stroked her neck. Cyril saw her distinctly male larynx.

"Adam's apple, baby. Adam's apple. Eves don't got 'em. Tits are cheap. That Adam's apple costs."

Cyril swallowed the last of the Jameson and shuddered.

"Was it James Joyce who said, 'I'm prepared to make a lifelong mistake'?"

She looked at him curiously then, as if he might have turned strange on her. "I dunno, honey."

"I may have."

She regarded him for a moment and then turned to look at herself in the corner mirror. "Thas fine honey. Look, I'm going to order me a pizza. You want some?"

Cyril shook his head.

"You can stay," she said, "but I'm really hungry."

She went across the hall, where there was a phone, and ordered her pizza, after telling him exactly what she was going to do. The door was unlocked across the hall, but there didn't seem to be anyone there. She left both doors open so he could listen and see her and not be afraid. Afraid was the least of what he was. While she was calling, Cyril wandered out into the hall and wandered down it. The music in the hall got very loud, strange electronic music against a background of drums, horns, cymbals, and what sounded like throat singing. The music was from the last door on the right, closest to the entry; the door was open now, and as he passed Cyril looked in.

There were a lot of them in there. It was hard to tell how many because they kept bouncing around, kids mostly but some weren't, and they were all moving. There was a lot of light in the room from the open windows and it seemed airy, even though there were a lot of mattresses crowded in there. Some were jumping on the mattresses and then rebounding from the walls. There was a lot of flung sweat and spiky black hair. They were Korean kids, he guessed, that made sense, but they could be Japanese. Many of them were wearing white headbands with Asian symbols, but some of them looked more like they had head wounds and had been bandaged. The red letters looked like blood. The effect was brave, like Kamikaze pilots photographed after their final sake. It seemed to be important to collide or nearly collide and gain new energy. They were like birds battering at each other, but with no sense of fear or entrapment like birds in a room would be. Cyril couldn't decide if they were drugged or religiously ecstatic. They bounded about the room insanely and didn't seem to care that he saw them. At the height of his bounce, one boy smiled or grimaced at Cyril and then his eyes rolled back as he dropped, shouting.

Outside, even though it was now rush hour, seemed peaceful.

Cyril thought about going back inside, but he decided that no one could have imagined that. Best to push on.

There was plenty of time left on the meter. Less than thirty minutes had passed, and that shocked him. Cyril put another quarter into the meter and set off walking. He found a quiet bar, Duffy's. Despite the name, the clientele seemed to be Central American, Guatemalan, Salvadorean, or even Honduran, he couldn't place the accent, and they were clearly worried about him, particularly after he ordered in Spanish. He was drinking Depth Charges now, shots of house whiskey dropped into a mug of draft beer. He didn't want to worry them in case they thought he was Migra. He wanted to reassure them. He would reassure them, but at the moment he desperately needed to piss. On his path to the bathroom, he walked through a small room with a pool table. It was like a room in a house with wall-to-wall burnt orange carpet. The pool table was nearly luminous under the overhead lights; the green felt and the scattered balls shimmered. "The Green Fire," Cyril said. The players cleared a path for him, chalking their cues and looking elsewhere, and he was reminded of his obligation to reassure them.

The room was empty when he came back, and so was most of the barroom. The bartender, wiping glasses, looked at him sourly. Cyril remembered his name, he always asked the name as he sat down, a salesman's habit. "José," Cyril said, "you have a really dirty rug back there." The bartender wiped Cyril's cleared space and nudged a neatly written tab to its center. "José," Cyril said, "I think I can help you."

VI. BAREFOOT SAINTS

When Cyril Cleary was fired by Encyclopedia Americana, he plunged into full-time debauchery with a sense of duty.

In the last two years he had also been fired by Hoover Vacuum Cleaners, Singer Sewing Machine, Schenkel Cutlery,
and Los Angeles Roofing, but Americana—bowdlerized
imitators of Encyclopedia Britannica—to be let go by the
likes of them was an inspiring low. Even his counselor at
the California State Employment office, after snorting at
Cyril's job description—*Door to door to door to door. Slam,
slam, slam, slam*—couldn't think of another option. Americana had been the last, where he sent his damaged cases.

A sad-eyed, ritually smiling man, Mr. Martell regarded Cyril's file for the appropriate duration, and then Cyril.
"Do you have any objections to physical labor?" he asked.
"I know you're well educated, but perhaps some physical
work would be good. Outdoors, put you back on your feet,
slow the drinking a bit."

Cyril studied Mr. Martell's sad eyes, swimming behind
his thick spectacles, his ridiculous stick arms floating from
his crepey, white short-sleeved shirt, the tremors of his
hands, and saw a fellow boozer. Mr. Martell's gaze dropped.
"Well, think about it. The only other thought I had was that
you might go back to the Church. My understanding is that
forgiveness is required by that institution." A rictus of a
smile. "Prodigal Son and all that." They left it there. Cyril went to collect his check at another desk belonging to a
large blond woman poised before a typewriter. She asked
his *exact name and spell it please so that I may correctly type
it*. When he did, the woman shied at his whiskey breath,
and her chins trembled with indignation as she handed the
state voucher to him.

His liquor store was pleased to cash the check. Mr.

Park, the successor to Mr. Kim at Lupe's Groceries, now Lupe's Liquors, delighted in stability, and government checks were the best. Cyril made concessions to his new budget. He refused the proffered fifth of his usual Jameson and asked for a quart of Old Crow, a savings of eight dollars. He brought a tallboy six-pack of Rainier Ale to the counter, a three-dollar savings over his beloved Guinness. He had already resolved to stay out of costly bars. He had only used them as a convenience between the door-to-door because he tried not to drink on the street while working. He wouldn't miss the people or the laggardly conversations he met there. He'd yet to find a philosopher or even a historian in an American bar. Unless the boxing was on, or soccer, and soccer was never on for long unless it was a Mexican bar, there wasn't much to talk about.

With these economies in place, he would have enough to refine his taste in whores. He scoured San Fernando Road and Eagle Rock Boulevard, sipping his ale with the Buick's windows down, so that he could converse with the women as they walked or sat on bus benches.

He was particular. He avoided the beautiful, the too young, the flashy, the well-dressed jaunty whores. Lightly soiled doves were once his choice, but his taste had darkened. Cyril drove miles, circling and funneling down, seeking out the wounded, the fluttering, the visibly damaged.

During the day, he would take them to Peliconi Park, and a small clearing hidden from the road where he would unroll the foam pad he kept tied in the trunk. At night, the Buick was their bedroom in one of the cul-de-sacs or giant shadowy parking lots Cyril favored. A very few complained that he was cheap, those who hoped for their kickback from the Hotsheets Motels of the neighborhood. He told them he hated landlords, on principle; if they complained enough or even agreed about landlords, he would add a few dollars to the tab, on principle.

Then, a miracle. His landlady in the front duplex, the relentless Mrs. Kessler, suffered a series of small strokes. That was Cyril's guess, it might be Alzheimer's, but the shift was sudden. Cyril became aware of the changes when he was collecting his newspaper and Mrs. Kessler, from her kitchen window, said what sounded like *Good morning* and then smiled at him, the first smile he had seen on her face in the two years he had lived there.

She began overfeeding her cat, to the point that the creature could scarcely waddle. The cat-food tins over-flowed the trash barrel and racoons arrived nightly to snack on the largesse.

The woman was clearly fuddled, but not in any dangerous way. She managed. Most importantly, Mrs. Kessler ceased asking for the rent, and Cyril stopped paying it. She also stopped monitoring his behavior. Previously, his step on the walk meant her stern face over folded arms, a skull and crossbones flying in that front window. Once she saw he had no company, she would turn away.

Now Mrs. Kessler wandered her rooms in cheerful disarray, sometimes vacuuming, washing, or cooking after midnight, never minding him. Cyril began bringing women home.

It was a voluptuous time. Sometimes he was so drunk that not much happened, sometimes the women were so high that the rites turned strange and vivid. He cherished the memory of Baby Doll, who trusted Cyril enough now to smoke crack in front of him. She was from Myrtle Beach, South Carolina, the daughter and granddaughter of army wives. "The first honest woman," Baby Doll said, "in three generations." She'd been one of the first whores he found, when he was so green that he attempted to give her pleasure, thumbing her clit while she rode him. "What are you doing?" she asked.

"I don't mind if you enjoy yourself," Cyril said.

"But I don't know you," she said. Cyril understood this was a truth, and that if he were ever to understand women, as much as any Irish man raised Catholic could, his education would begin there.

He had stopped seeing her for a time. She was too pretty and had a wise mouth. When she saw him on the street, and she taught the other whores to say it too, she would call out his mantra: "Forty bucks and I come twice."

Now she was well-worn by the street and would sometimes spend the night with Cyril, at no extra charge. On the night that he cherished, she arrived at his door with a black plastic bag of clothes, a clear zippered pouch crammed with makeup, a handled paper bag filled with shoes and aerosol cans of hair spray, and, balled in foil, stuffed in the toe of a single yellow pump, two large rocks of cocaine. He understood this to mean that she was no longer wasting money on rent. She offered him some of the crack and he turned her down as always. That was another thing she liked about him.

Baby Doll smoked her first rock and allowed him to

pour her some ale, to temper the high. By two o'clock, she'd smoked a quarter of the second rock, firing her glass pipe until the bowl turned cherry, while her thin chest swelled with the smoke and her eyes bulged. Then Baby Doll turned bizarre. What stayed with him was that she seemed to have an idea in mind. He looked down to see her spraying Aqua Net hair spray on his cock. He'd answered the door in a T-shirt and socks, but he'd forgotten until now that he was pantless. The cold sticky spray stung a little and the sharp odor of industrial alcohol filled his nose and watered his eyes. She sucked him hard and they fucked for the first time, with her groaning and hammering on his clenched buttocks with her tiny fists. When he asked about the hair spray, she said, "Next time I'll light your dick on fire and put it out with my pusseah." *Pussy* was the only word she still pronounced South Carolina–style. She knew it amused him.

The evening descended to mumbles and twitches and frantic searches for increasingly small shards of crack that had to be combed from the carpet.

He was awakened the next day by the afternoon light entering his wide-open front door. Her clothes were gone and so were two books he'd been reading, one on the Peloponnesian wars, the other on the murder of Lorca, but the can of hair spray remained, set on a plate in the middle of the floor.

Two letters arrived, one inside the other. The first was from his mother in Ireland, folded inside the other, from his former principal at St. Patrick's, Brother Malachy.

His mother was distraught. *Where are you?* she wrote in her crabbed and perfect hand, the craft of long-dead nuns. *Have you left the order? My last letter was returned to me. They said you were not known at that address.* She went on to say she loved him and would respect any decision he had made and then wrote another two pages explaining what a mistake it would be to leave the Church and why he wouldn't be forgiven at home and why she couldn't tell anyone or now even make a good confession.

When he'd left the order, two years before, he'd reached an understanding with Brother Malachy. "She's an old woman," Cyril told him. "The news might kill her. At the least, it would make her last days miserable. There's a continent and an ocean between us, and she has never left County Clare in her lifetime. She would never find out unless we tell her."

Brother Malachy had asked, "Then you don't plan to visit home?" When Cyril admitted that no, he had no plans to see Ireland, Malachy agreed. Cyril understood that Malachy had hopes for his return, he had been a favorite. For the next two years Malachy had forwarded Mother Cleary's letters to Cyril, and Cyril had written faithfully back, about how well the school was doing, of his hopes for the basketball team, the praise he'd received from the principal, and Bishop Manning's visit to consecrate the new school chapel.

Brother Malachy's letter explained what had happened. *I am sorry to tell you that while I was away to St. Catherine's on a retreat, a letter arrived from your mother. I am afraid that Brother Ivar seized the opportunity. I believe that he refused to accept the letter from the postman and indicated you no longer live here. Your mother has written to*

me and asked if this is true. I think we must talk. Please call
me and we shall make an appointment.

Cyril put down the letter. That lickspittle wormy shite,
Ivar. Of course it was and of course he did. He'd hated Cyril
since that pugilistic embarrassment in the seminary. Two
teeth and the broken nose. Improved his horse face. And
when Cyril had left, the bastard had the temerity to say he
would pray for him.

Cyril rang the rectory doorbell and listened to the
chimes. It was strange standing before a door he'd always
walked through. He waited in the dim entry, watching
moths bat against the overhead light. Brother Malachy
opened the door and greeted Cyril warmly, with an embrace
and kiss to the cheek. It was just eight o'clock, the time
Cyril had requested because he wished to appear employed.
He had prepared carefully, his good suit, close shave, and
fresh haircut. He had eaten an early dinner and he had not
drunk at all that day, only a Guinness.

Brother Malachy had a fire crackling against the cool
evening in the snug common room and he uncorked the
Jameson and poured them both a dollop. They tossed those
off, ceremonially, and Malachy spilled larger measures and
they sat comfortably in the green velveteen chairs cocked
toward the fire. Cyril could see that Malachy was alight
with enthusiasm, which was a worry.

Malachy lifted his glass so the firelight caught it. "Better days," he said. "I've been thinking on this. Your dear
mother and the situation. I have to ask first, are you happy
in your work?"

Warily, Cyril approached the topic: "It suits." He saw

Malachy was studying his face. "It's steady." Clearly, that wasn't enough. "They're good books. Definitive."

An eyebrow arched in response. "You're no longer selling the vacuum machines, then?"

"No," Cyril said. "Encyclopedias. Britannica. The best in the field."

Malachy sipped. "Selling the store of the world's knowledge. You're still an educator, then."

"It's a job," Cyril said, "not a calling."

Malachy pounced. "Here's what I'll propose. We're losing Brother Robert. He's inherited a house and his father's stable and is going home. History, Senior English, Honors English, Latin, and Spanish, that's his schedule. You've taught all but the History before. I'm not asking you to rejoin the order. We would bring you back as a lay teacher. It would be good to have you back. Good for you, too, I think."

Cyril put down his drink. "I can't teach."

Malachy leaned forward. "You were a great teacher. Of course you can teach. You're saying you won't teach."

"No," Cyril said, "I can't teach."

"Of course you *can*," Malachy said, and Cyril remembered him, chewing on the debate team—*Define your terms, gentlemen. Clarity*—"Why *won't* you?" Malachy asked.

Cyril stood. "When you teach, you're offering hope."

"Hope...possibilities, you offer the world," Malachy said. "Sit back down. Finish your drink."

"That means, the teacher has to draw from a store, that hope. Like Starbuck's courage." Cyril spoke carefully now, he felt his brogue returning, the urge to declaim, and checked it. "To teach, you have to have hope. I don't have that."

He turned away and walked for the door, knowing he was startling Malachy, who was disposed to gnaw on an idea. Malachy sent up his last rocket. "What shall I tell your mother?"

"Tell her what you like," Cyril said, "and don't send me the auld bitch's letters." He couldn't help the brogue. The door clicked shut behind him, and as he walked to his gleaming Buick, washed yesterday for the first time that year, he caught a flicker of movement behind the firelit window. There was the smash of a glass and then Malachy's furious voice. "Bloody lunatics. Bloody romantics! Goddamn Irish!"

Cyril searched for Baby Doll. On San Fernando Road, York Avenue, and Eagle Rock Boulevard, among the forced gaiety of rival car lots with their overhead lines of twirling propellers and streaming tinsel, where she had perched herself on hoods and fenders, behind the taco trucks that provided cover and late-night drunken customers, at all the select bus benches at prominent intersections where she had crossed and recrossed her legs with each orange and red light, Cyril looked for Baby Doll and asked after her among the working girls. It had been almost two weeks since she'd left him her hair spray, and he hadn't found her again.

At Baby Doll's favored corner of Eagle Rock Boulevard and Fletcher, at a bus bench that had once been her staked territory, Cyril shared the fresh cheese pupusas he had brought with two Salvadoran whores, Esperanza and Marisol.

He'd known them both for more than a year and had

watched them evolve from skinny, scared new girls to doughy veteranas. He hired them when there was no one interesting around and he was ready to settle for a business transaction. They were businesswomen. Neither drank nor drugged. Both were building houses back in El Salvador and carried photos of their construction. Marisol's was a two-story cinderblock with so many arched windows it looked like an arcade. Marisol was the designer, her brother-in-law was the carpenter, and he built the whims she sketched and paid for. Stucco and paint had been applied in the most recent photos, and the house now looked like a pink-and-white frosted cake, with cracks and fissures already visible in the swirled creamy surface.

Passing the photos back, Cyril asked about Baby Doll. The two women looked at each other. Marisol sat down on the bus bench. "She sleeping," Esperanza said.

"Sleeping?" Cyril said. Marisol pressed her hands together, tilted and rested her head against them as though they were a pillow, and closed her eyes. "Baby Doll sleeping," she said.

He asked them again in Spanish, and Marisol repeated her tableau, eyelids fluttering, her face softening into repose. "Ella esta sueño," Esperanza whispered, and Cyril finally understood they were telling him Baby Doll was dead, in a way that spoke no ill of the dead nor drew any bad luck to their lives.

Cyril brought home a woman he hadn't seen on the boulevard before. She was sitting on the bus bench at the corner of Fletcher and San Fernando. It was after two; he was drunk and had been thrown out of the Tiki Ti for presumption. He needed a small victory. He asked if she wanted a ride. She seemed slightly dazed and took a long time to respond. "I guess," she said, and he leaned to push open the door. It wasn't until she was in the car that he realized she wasn't wearing shoes.

She had a sweet, round, agreeable face, and that seemed to be her nature as well. She said her name was Dawn, though later she would remember it was Debi with an i.

Back at the house, Mrs. Kessler was seated at her dining room table, stirring something in a metal bowl. Her huge marmalade cat was on the table, his nose at the rim of the bowl, eyes following her fist and the wooden spoon. Behind them, Mrs. Kessler's old upright vacuum cleaner howled.

Once in the door at his place, Cyril offered Dawn a drink. "I'd like some water," she said. "Please." She drank it down and began to take her clothes off. She was wearing an oversize dark navy wrap dress, and that was all she was wearing. She rolled the dress, put it on the floor for a pillow, and then laid back flat on the rug. Her hands grasped her knees and she opened her legs.

Cyril stared at the upraised soles of her feet. They were black and crusted. She lay there, legs open, eyes closed, face in repose. A still life, behind her a spilled pile of library books, on the dresser scattered change and two empties of Rainier Ale, a folded paper plate, a box of chicken bones, and his unmade bed, covered with unpacked laundry in blue paper and the week's newspapers.

Drunk as he was, he understood he had reached bottom. He hadn't thought there was one, not for him. It was her meekness, he thought. He touched the blackened sole of her left foot. "Never mind," Cyril said. It was like touching a lump of coal. "I'll still give you the money." She lowered her free leg, her eyes remained closed. He held her foot and studied the cracked and riven sole, then thumbed it. A loamy odor reached him.

The word came to him, *discalced*, from the Latin—*dis*, without, *calceus*, shoe—the discalced Carmelites, the discalced Franciscans. The barefoot saints, Francis and Clare. "Discalced Dawn," Cyril said. Her eyes opened then. "It's Debi," she said, "with an i. I thought you might be a cop."

He got her to accept a pair of his sweat socks and old tennis shoes, but she wouldn't put them on. She set them down on the bus bench, when they reached it, and sat beside them. He gave Debi the money, though he knew he didn't need to. She folded her fingers over the bills when he pressed them on her palm, but she never looked at them.

Cyril slowly circled the block in his Buick, sipping at his last bit of whiskey. The third time round she was gone and the socks were gone, but the shoes remained. Cyril left them there and drove to St. Patrick's.

Brother Malachy sat up and looked at his bedside clock; it was just after 4:30, still dark out. The house was still and there was nothing troubling him. He wondered why he was awake.

From the train yards across San Fernando Road came the idling murmur and then the strain of switch engines, distant whistles and horns, but these noises had never wakened him; if anything they soothed him, kept him asleep.

He went to the dining room window. A light burned at the school, the sixth floor. Malachy slipped on his cassock and shoes. He took up the knobbed ceremonial shillelagh.

The school was open, a key still in the front door lock. Malachy crept up the stairs, avoiding the noise and warning of the elevator.

The light was from the chapel. Its doors were thrown open, lights shone down on the empty pews, and the wooden altar blazed with candles. The altar rail gates were open, and face down, just outside the breach, was Cyril. His bare feet gleamed. Malachy's heart lurched.

Malachy leaned the shillelagh against the doorway. He dipped his hand in the holy water font, crossed himself and then genuflected toward the tabernacle. He walked processionally down the middle aisle. As he approached Cyril, he could see the rise and fall of his breathing and then heard the light snoring. Malachy's shoulders lowered, and he nodded his head in thanks.

The placement and attitude of Cyril's body was familiar to Malachy, to anyone who had been ordained. His body flattened, his arms outflung in the shape of the Cross, Cyril was prostrated. It was the last posture of the novice, before approaching the altar to make his vows.

Malachy gathered Cyril's brown moccasins and tan socks. He rolled the socks and tucked them in the shoes. Malachy set the shoes down on the carpeted step outside the altar rail and knelt beside them.

EMILIANO PART IV: RIDE THE BLACK HORSE

IN THE EARLY morning, Emiliano saw a hawk crouched on the phone pole. It was an immature redtail, a female—still yellow billed and speckled—but a big, chesty bird. The tail feathers held only the palest hint of red. She stood on the crossbar at the top of the pole, shoulders bunched, bringing her heavy wings up close to her head. Four mockingbirds flapped and darted around the hawk in a shifting halo, yelling like fledglings. The hawk called regularly, a muted, protesting *"skreee."* Between calls her beak gaped and the vibrating tongue protruded as if she were panting.

It wasn't uncommon to see a hawk harried by mockingbirds, particularly now, in nesting season, but this hawk's behavior intrigued Emiliano. Hawks seldom settled when harried. This one might be hurt or, because she was young and inexperienced, had been driven down to the pole, but it seemed odd to Emiliano. The hawk hunched and swayed like a boxer but stayed resolutely on the crossbar. The mockingbirds plunged and nipped at her fanned tail feathers. The hawk ruffled and shuddered but stayed. She called continually. It seemed odd.

In the afternoon, after his can of soup, Emiliano walked up the hill toward Peliconi Park. It had been a strange morning. The hawk had flown off around ten when the mockingbirds had tired of their sport. Just after that, all the neighborhood dogs started to howl.

Emiliano thought at first that there must be a new dog. That was the usual reason. Put twenty-five dogs in twenty-five backyards, they worked it out. Add one dog and the new scent in the breeze would drive them all crazy. They would howl and bark—even Mrs. Espinosa's tired Chihuahua would totter out from his basket and yap at the screen—until they'd redivided this new territory. Barking diplomats, Emiliano thought. It was the way borders were drawn.

This howling was different. The dogs ignored each other and barked and howled like mourners. Emiliano had heard them bay like this only once before, during an eclipse. He was walking up Salsipuedes Street when the barking stopped. It didn't stop the way it usually did, with yips and grumbles and the delayed chant of the dumbest dog that hadn't got the airborne message. They stopped all at once. Emiliano turned around and looked down the hill. The silence was startling, more than just quiet. The neighborhood was quieter than it could be, like a theater audience that concentrates and absorbs any sound that might distract.

Emiliano paused, resting on his cane, waiting for the neighborhood to come back to life. On San Fernando Road a cement truck ground away from a stoplight and the one o'clock buzzer droned at the pallet factory, but the neighborhood stayed still. He waited. At the pallet factory, the saws whined to life and the gasp and thwack of nail guns punctured the still air. From the west he heard the faint scree and saw of slow trains on curved rails and the thudding concussion of a freight braking on a siding. He started walking again.

All the way up Salsipuedes Street, Emiliano saw the silent dogs, some crouched and panting, others yearning with muzzles poked through hedges and gates, or humble, leaned toward one another at their fences. All of them were waiting, Emiliano thought; it reminded him of his visit to Guadalupe and the pilgrims there, shy but sure that the Virgin would appear to honor their particular faith. Like the pilgrims, the dogs' eyes were black with fervor, or anticipation.

At the last house on Salsipuedes, where Luis Romero and his family had re-created the lost family ranchito in Guerrero—a hillside garden of cactus, chayote twined around cornstalks, rusted barbed wire fencing, and bougainvillea—where he was usually greeted by three happy mutts and scratching chickens, nothing moved. Today the dogs were hiding and the chickens had gone to roost. The rooster stared at him, from the shadows under the coop.

The trail veered out toward the edge, and as always he caught his first glimpse of Elysian Park and Dodger Stadium, and as always Emiliano crossed himself, offered a prayer to the memory of his Aunt Lupe, and thought about the curse she'd put on Chavez Ravine.

As Emiliano reached the top of the hill, the entrance to Peliconi Park, he was struck by the stillness of the air; the light was yellow and hazy. The Scotch broom, the wild tobacco, and fennel that surrounded the park green stood straight and still.

Below him, beyond the train yards and the concrete slot of the Los Angeles River, the 5 freeway hummed until the right lanes slowed for the Pasadena Freeway juncture. The sycamores and oaks on the hillsides of Elysian Park, usually moving in the afternoon breeze, were still, and so were the eucalyptus next to the police academy and the palms surrounding Dodger Stadium.

Almost as soon as he thought it—*earthquake weather*—the earth around him and below him started to roll. The noise was like thunder compressed into a crack. It was only the second time he had been high enough to look down on an earthquake. The first time had been when he was five, visiting his legendary grandfather in Zacatecas, and as the mountains danced around him and his grandmother and mother and sisters had screamed, his grandfather had snatched him out from under the table where Emiliano had gone to hide. "¡Montemos al caballo negro!" his grandfather had commanded. He'd dragged Emiliano to the milpa beside the house, where he'd yanked up cornstalks by the handful and made Emiliano tug up a cornstalk by himself. When the shaking stopped, he'd stomped back to the houseful of wailing women, bearing the cornstalks aloft, Emiliano trailing his own stalk.

"You see," his grandfather had said. "You only have to pull on the god's hair to make him stop."

This god wasn't stopping. Emiliano had never lived through a quake this long. The freeways looked like gray snakes rippling upward. Windows started to break in the streets below him, bursting outward as though shot. The hills groaned and pounded. Car alarms brayed, burglar alarms clanged and shrilled. Railroad cars started to topple in chains; craters of dirt sprayed up around each car as it hit. On the freeway, a truck towing two silver beetle-shaped tanks tweaked and separated and cars slid sideways to the margins. The hills of Elysian Park humped and twisted.

The Los Angeles River bottom jolted to face him with the water pouring down, and then the concrete channel cracked and as far as he could see rocks, rubble, and slabs popped into the air and descended into dusty clouds.

Emiliano clutched at a yucca beside him and rode the rock and sway. Clearly, Shaky Town, which had always suffered most in each previous quake, was being favored. This time the hills opposite bore the brunt, and as Emiliano clung and watched, the promontory of Chavez Ravine and Dodger Stadium tilted into view and then cracked. There was no other word for it. Chavez Ravine stood up on end like a bowl held aloft, and he could see the blue and yellow seats of the upper decks cascading down into the outfield like poker chips onto felt.

"¡Montemos al caballo negro!" his grandfather had commanded, and Emiliano, holding onto the yucca, waved an arm and shouted, "Ride the black horse!" The rolling waves subsided to surges, then twitches, then tremors, then stillness as vast clouds of dust swelled from the new valley of Elysian Park, and the first flames started to rise.

He sank to his knees, and as the quiet grew he heard honking, the first sirens, and then laughter that seemed to be inside his head, but it wasn't his grandfather, and he said aloud, "Aunt Lupe. What have you done?"

ACKNOWLEDGMENTS

I have been misreading a line from William Wordsworth for thirty years. *Child is father of the Man,* Wordsworth wrote. Most scholars agree that Wordsworth was saying that who you were as a child, will be who you become as an adult. As a teacher, I've always read this line differently. I think it means that as you age, your students should eclipse you and eventually become your mentors. That has certainly happened to me with this book. I am forever indebted to Jim Gavin, who made it possible.

The second person who made it possible is my wife, Alison Turner, who worked to provide me with the time to write *Shaky Town* and six other books.

Finally, thank you to everybody else. There have been some wonderful writers, artists and editors who helped along the way. You know who you are.

ABOUT THE AUTHOR

LOU MATHEWS has written seven books and published two of them, *Just Like James* and *L.A. Breakdown*, which was a *Los Angeles Times* Best Book. He has taught in UCLA Extension's acclaimed creative writing program since 1989. His stories have been published in *ZYZZYVA*, *New England Review*, *Short Story*, *Black Clock*, *Paperback L.A.*, and many fiction anthologies. Mathews is also a journalist, playwright, and passionate cook, as well as a former mechanic, street racer, and restaurant critic. He has received a Pushcart Prize and a Katherine Anne Porter Prize, as well as California Arts Commission and NEA Fiction fellowships, and is a recipient of the UCLA Extension Teacher of the Year and Outstanding Instructor awards.

.